THE AMERICA COLLECTION 8: SHE LOVES ME, SHE LOVES ME NOT

Dixie Lynn Dwyer

MENAGE EVERLASTING

Siren Publishing, Inc.
www.SirenPublishing.com

A SIREN PUBLISHING BOOK
IMPRINT: Ménage Everlasting

THE AMERICAN SOLDIER COLLECTION 8: SHE LOVES ME, SHE LOVES ME NOT

ISBN: 978-1-62741-947-5

First Printing: September 2014

Cover design by Les Byerley

Printed in the U.S.A.

PUBLISHER
Siren Publishing, Inc.
www.SirenPublishing.com

DEDICATION

Dear loyal readers, thank you for purchasing this legal copy of *The American Soldier Collection 8: She Loves Me, She Loves Me Not.*

How do you take a chance when you're so fearful? Can love really conquer all life throws at you, just as time tests everyone's vulnerability? Can relying so much on others cause you to lose yourself? When the attraction is so strong, the bond incredibly pure, and the fears similarly shared by those you're taking a chance on, is it worth it in the end?

Taking that chance, gaining that strength may help you face what's yet to come. Having others alongside you, lending support, experiencing the same risks, may just be powerful enough to conquer it all.

Join Ellie, Mace, Hunter, Seno, and Justice as they face the demons of their pasts, and learn to take a chance on love, on vulnerability, and ultimately their last shot at happiness.

Happy Reading!

Hugs!

~Dixie~

THE AMERICAN SOLDIER COLLECTION 8: SHE LOVES ME, SHE LOVES ME NOT

DIXIE LYNN DWYER

Prologue

Ellie Morrison walked into the board meeting with confidence and attitude. She'd landed this job because she was creative, thought out of the box, and loved people. Her boss, Ernest, was not easy to please. But when most rubbed him the wrong way, Ellie seemed to say and do exactly what he expected from a loyal, capable employee.

She still felt self-conscious when men checked her out or tried to flirt, and especially in the workplace. Her therapist, Kate Rutherford, told her it would take time for that anxiety to ease. It had been four months since Paul assaulted her, and a year and six months since she lost her uncle Brian, her only relative, in a robbery gone badly.

She swallowed hard, tapped the stack of manila folders filled with the documents she'd worked on for weeks just for this meeting today.

"Gentlemen, it brings me great pleasure to present to you today, our ideas for the launch of your new state-of-the-art restaurant franchise." She started to hand out the folders, and the seven men watched her, nodded, and took the folders. They opened them immediately, and she saw the instant surprise and, she hoped, excitement in their eyes.

"Miss Morrison, these are quite extraordinary ideas," Luke Phillips said. He was Renaldo Sentinel's right-hand man, his personal assistant, and his bodyguard. Renaldo was an entrepreneur, a multimillionaire with hands in many different businesses including imports and exports. He had wanted to incorporate some specific things that portrayed his personal love, in each restaurant. It hadn't been easy to come up with an idea that would still be appealing to the eye and not so overdone with artwork.

"Well, Mr. Phillips, Mr. Sentinel wanted to incorporate some Venetian artwork into the restaurants. There are many bold colors, very detailed images that could be used throughout the restaurants without being overpowering. These are just preliminary ideas, but I am certain we can find exactly what Mr. Sentinel is looking for," she stated.

Renaldo Sentinel watched her intently. He was a very attractive man, with black slicked-back hair, and deep gray eyes. He was definitely an eye-catcher, and boy did he know it. In the short period of time she had known him, she had seen him with five different women. It was obvious that the bachelor was a ladies' man.

"I'm not certain this is what Renaldo is looking for," Luke added.

"Luke, I think that Ellie has done a wonderful job. I like the ideas, but I'm not certain on the preliminary architectural designs. Venetian art can be incorporated in numerous ways. However, I do prefer the more eye-catching images. Scenes of people in action, the gondolas, the masks and brilliant gold color. Perhaps it would serve you well, Ellie, to accompany me to Tratorra's. This Saturday, seven o'clock good for you? I can have my driver pick you up."

She wasn't completely shocked. She was used to Mr. Sentinel's controlling ways. But she wasn't going to fall into instant obedience. After all, she didn't want him thinking that she could be his next fling. So she followed her gut.

"I'll have to check my schedule. I'll call Luke later today. Now how about we get back to the files, and discuss the numbers. I believe they will be more than satisfactory and most importantly below your budget limit. That being said, we should still have room for any potential cosmetic changes."

Renaldo stared at her, and Luke, well, he just seemed annoyed.

"We can discuss it over dinner, Saturday. I'll have my people look over the contracts and I'll sign them then so we can get moving on construction and so forth," he said, standing up, ending the meeting minutes after it only got started.

She felt as if the wind was knocked out of her and one look at her boss and she saw that he was just as shocked.

"Don't you have more questions?" Ernest Westerly, asked, rising so he could shake Renaldo's hand good-bye.

Renaldo smiled and looked at Ellie. "If I have any questions, I'm certain that Ellie will be able to answer them. I must go now. I have another meeting across town in thirty minutes." He left the room with his entourage, leaving Ellie, Ernest, and three other employees standing there in shock.

"That man has got a set on him," Cecile stated with an attitude as she grabbed her laptop and binder before heading out of the room.

"Why didn't you accept his invite to dinner, Ellie? A lot is riding on this contract. Three million dollars," Ernest stated.

She looked at him as she gathered up her stuff. "Earnest, need I remind you that I'm not a perk to doing business with this firm."

"Ellie, you know that's not what I mean. Of course you're not. I mean, it's obvious that he likes you, and well, he is a very well-known man."

"Please. I'm not interested. I don't date, remember?" She started to walk from the room.

"We need this contract, Ellie. We're one job away from laying off workers because it's been so slow. If we land this job, we're set for quite some time, never mind the publicity we'll get, which means more high profile clients."

She knew that construction and development firm was struggling. But they were still pretty well off.

"I'm still not going to lead him on in order to get this gig. He said he would sign the contracts."

"Yes, at dinner with you Saturday night. Clear your schedule. Although I know you don't have any plans."

"Fine. I'll clear my schedule, and I'll go out with Renaldo, but if I get us this contract, I expect one hefty bonus check for snagging this job. And I mean big, Ernest. I don't like playing games, and I certainly don't like being bossed around." She gave him a stern expression and then headed out of the room wondering how the hell she got herself into this.

Chapter 1

"I said that I'm fine. Just leave me the hell alone!" Hunter yelled at his brothers before limping from the room.

Justice ran his fingers through his wavy blond hair, and then looked at Seno and Mace, his younger siblings.

"I don't get it. Is it me or is his attitude getting worse again?" Justice asked.

"It's getting worse again. He's in pain from overdoing it at the gym. You know that puts him in a wicked mood," Seno said, and then poured the rest of his coffee down the drain.

"I thought he was past trying to prove himself to the world. What happened to Ray Anne?" Justice asked.

Mace snorted. "That bitch. I didn't like her at all. I could tell that she was using him."

"Hell, Mace, we know that she was using him but figured he was using her, too. It's not easy for him to just jump into bed with any woman. Not with his hang-up about his leg."

"Justice, we've seen the signs before. The self-destruction, the drinking, the pushing over the limit. We don't need him relapsing. Quantum won't take him back into the unit if Hunter fucks this up again," Mace stated.

Justice thought about that a moment. If it weren't for Quantum, the whole lot of them wouldn't even be alive right now. Their team leader, their commander from the military, helped Justice, Seno, and Mace to save Hunter when he was captured and tortured by insurgents. Hunter had survived a roadside bomb when the rest of his team hadn't. Then he was dragged through the streets and held captive for three weeks. It took Quantum and some friends in the government to locate Hunter and then to initiate a secret plan to go in and get him out of there. Justice, Seno, and Mace would never forget that mission, or the heartache and the difficulty they faced seeing their brother, the youngest of the four of them, cut up, bloodied, and dying. They all had the scars to prove that mission took place, but Hunter had the ultimate one, a prosthetic leg.

"I'll talk to him in a little while. You know, try to settle him down, find out about Ray Anne. We also have plans to meet Quentin, Axel, Deacon, and L.T. at Casper's tonight," Mace reminded him.

"Oh yeah, damn, I forgot about that. Quentin called last night and said that Mariah and her friends were meeting for drinks at Ray Ray's down the street and then would head over to Casper's," Justice added.

"I'm surprised they even let Mariah out of their sights," Mace stated and chuckled. They all did.

"Like you wouldn't act the same way if you had a girlfriend who looked like Mariah and after everything she went through and was nearly killed?" Justice asked. He felt that twinge of need in his chest. He and his brothers were close, but their lives, their pasts were so fucked up they feared intimacy. That was why they never took any woman seriously and pretty much stayed away from the ones who wanted to latch on. It was easier to not feel anything than it was to risk feeling something for a woman only for her to let him down. There wasn't a woman he could count on, but his brothers he always could.

"You're right. If we found the perfect woman who had all the qualities and things we each desired, she'd be right beside one of us at all times or at minimum in bed where we could thoroughly keep an eye on her," Mace stated.

Seno laughed. "That didn't quite work out with Renee did it, bro?" Seno teased Mace.

"Renee was fun, and I enjoyed the time we spent together but she wasn't right for us," Mace replied.

"She was never right for you either," Justice added.

That bitch was so rude to Hunter. She made comments about his prosthetic, and about him not being whole. Justice was glad that Mace saw through her hurtful, true colors and got rid of her. A lot of women were like that. Superficial, not empathetic, and just not knowledgeable of the mental and physical difficulties involved with having a prosthetic leg. Their brother was whole, and he was more than capable of handling anything any of the rest of them could handle. Proving that all the time led to days like today when Hunter was in pain from overdoing it at work and helping to train other soldiers like himself to defend themselves minus a limb or two.

"Yeah, definitely talk to him and calm him down, or he's going to be hell to deal with tonight at Casper's," Justice stated.

They were all quiet for a minute until Mace spoke. "Do you even think it's possible to find someone who could accept Hunter for who he is?"

Justice looked at Mace and then Seno. "Oh, I think it's possible, but I'm starting to wonder if Hunter can ever open himself up to that kind of vulnerability and allow someone in. He's been stuck in a wounded, defensive soldier state of mind for more than three years now. It's going to take a miracle and someone with a hell of a lot of courage to break him down."

"Thanks for knocking the wind out of my sails, Justice," Mace replied.

Seno snorted. "A woman as perfect as that may not exist, and we may need to make the decision none of us have been wanting to make."

"I'm not giving up on Hunter. We didn't back down then when they said to forget about him, that he was as good as dead. I'm sure as hell not giving up on him now. He'll come around, and if we find that woman we've been hoping to find for us to share and feel complete with, then Hunter will have to be part of it. It's the kind of relationship that would work best for all of us just as it has for our friends. Soldiers who have been what we've been through, brothers who've served in the field of battle like we did don't know any other way but together, one team one unit."

"Agreed. We give him more time. Besides, my money is on us growing old with no woman than finding one who can put up with the three of your bullshit," Mace told them.

"Our bullshit?" Seno asked, sounding insulted.

"Sure. Justice is a fucking control freak who has to be in charge and tell everyone what their purpose and job is. You're a fucking anal perfectionist who analyzes criminals to profile them for the government so your mind is never able to focus on relaxing and just giving your all to the moment. Hunter has a piss-poor attitude, and he takes out his anger training hand-to-hand combat and conducting computer analysis for hours and hours at a time. I'm the most normal of all of you," Mace stated.

"Normal? You call yourself fucking normal?" Seno asked.

"Your infatuation with everything John Wayne is fucking weird," Justice teased.

"Hey, John Wayne was a fucking cool guy. There's nothing weird about being a collector," Mace replied in defense.

"You paid five thousand dollars for one of his autographed pictures," Seno replied.

"You also collect those damn swords and knives. Your entire room looks like a vault for weaponry," Justice added.

"Hey, I like to collect certain things. I think John Wayne was awesome. I also like knives, and swords mean a lot to me after the years I spent training in sword fighting."

Seno and Justice chuckled as Mace went on defending himself while they headed out to work. They always teased one another. It was part of the close bond they all shared. The only difference was that now it seemed Hunter participated less and less and seemed to isolate himself more and more. Justice was at his wit's end. If he could have one wish granted in life it would be that his brother Hunter could feel whole again, and like a real man instead of an invalid, the way he seemed to really feel deep inside.

* * * *

Ellie waited to park her silver 1970 Corvette Stingray in a front spot that opened up in front of Ray Ray's bar. She eased it into the spot as she noticed a couple of guys checking out the car. It was an eye-catcher and a classic, left to her by her uncle Brian in his will. She loved the car, and Uncle Brian knew that since they shared a lot of Sunday afternoons together riding around. She turned off the ignition and looked at the front of Ray Ray's. It was an older bar frequented by lots of people in the police department as well as retirees. Her uncle Brian had hung out there often along with Uncle Reggie, whom everyone called Unc.

Unc wasn't her real uncle, but had taken on the responsibility of one, or at least the closest thing she had to an uncle besides Brian. They were best friends and had been partners in the police department for years. When Uncle Brian died in the store robbery, Ellie had taken it hard. So hard that she couldn't even function. It had been the worst thing to happen to her or so she thought until Paul came along.

Ellie sighed. Paul Lewis was a correctional officer. Fresh out of college and eyes wide open at the prospects a good-paying position could give her, she fell right into Paul's more mature and experienced personality. He was gorgeous, came from a wealthy family, very tough and demanding. He was also into some things she hadn't realized until it had nearly been too late.

She closed her eyes and pushed away the fearful thoughts. That was a year and a half ago. At least now when she saw Paul, she didn't have a panic attack. What he had done to her ruined any chances of her being with another man. At least she didn't think she could be intimate with someone any time soon.

She gathered her purse, and looked in the mirror to check her makeup. She could only stop to visit Unc for a little while. She had plans of going out with her roommates tonight, and she definitely wanted to change out of the business attire.

After getting out of the car and locking the doors, she headed inside. It was pretty crowded already for happy hour. She clutched her bag tightly against her belly as she saw the multiple eyes turn to look at her. She scanned the room for Unc and immediately saw Ray.

"Ellie, come on in, doll." He greeted her with a hug and then kisses to her cheek.

"Hello, Ray. How are you?"

"Doing well, how are you? Feeling okay? How is work?" he asked as he led her over toward the back of the room where Unc sat talking to some guy. He didn't look too happy but then Unc looked up and his face lit up. He was a great man, and a faithful friend to Uncle Brian. Unc had basically taken over Uncle Brian's role.

"Hey, Ellie, you made it. I thought you might not," Unc said as he stood up, dismissing the man who was sitting with him as the man walked away. Unc pulled her into his arms.

"I told you that I would make it."

Unc was tall, about six feet, with dark hair and only a bit of gray showing here and there. He was in his fifties, and in great physical condition, just like her uncle Brian had been.

"Come and sit down, join me for a while." He pulled out the chair and she sat down, smiling at him. She felt better having someone whom she thought of as family to sit down with and talk to. Although she had her three roommates, Moira, Donella and Jessie, too, this was different. Unc was like a father figure, and she felt lucky to have him.

"So, work must be pretty busy. You had to cancel lunch a few times." He leaned back and took a sip of his soda. Ray brought over a glass of club soda with lemon and winked as he placed it down in front of her before heading back to the bar.

She stirred the straw and looked at Unc. She didn't want to worry him about her business meeting tomorrow with Renaldo. Unc had been very protective of her along with Uncle Brian after Paul had assaulted her. She didn't dare tell him about Paul sending her a text message the other day trying to act as if he were forgiven.

"Something is bothering you. What's wrong? Tell me."

"It's nothing. It's just the same old problem I think I'll always have."

He looked concerned. "Has someone asked you out?"

She shook her head and his concern softened.

"Well, what then?"

"It's nothing really. I'm just still so paranoid about men, I guess. I'm wondering when I'll get over these feelings."

"You'll get over them when you meet someone perfect. Someone who will treat you the way you deserve to be treated."

She snorted in disbelief. "I wonder if there is any such person out there. And if there is, how will I know? I can't even trust myself, and my reaction to even an innocent conversation with a man. It's just not fair. Maybe Kate is right, and it's time to give dating a chance."

"You're still seeing her? I thought the therapy sessions were finished."

"They are, but she said I can call her whenever I needed to talk. In fact, I saw her last week while I was jogging down by the park."

He took another sip of his soda.

"I don't think there's any reason to rush into dating. If you meet someone and you're attracted to them, then make the decision to get to know them. But don't go out tonight with your friends with intentions of finding a guy. That can only lead to disaster."

"I'm not Donella. What she did a few weeks ago was stupid. She didn't know that guy. He said all the right things and made her feel special. She forgot the rules and about taking precautions. Who would have known the guy slipped her some ecstasy?"

"You knew. You had to get her away from that guy and then call me. She was out of it, and it was pretty damn scary."

"Yeah well, I just hope that guy, Leo, doesn't show up anywhere around these parts again. We couldn't prove that he put the drug in her drink, but I know Donella, and she was out of it. Some other unsuspecting female could become his next prey."

"I doubt it. There was no sign of him anywhere, and the police never located him. But still, you young ladies need to take precautions."

"I know, Unc. That was enough to scare all my friends."

She looked down at her lap and thought about the text from Paul. It made her feel guilty and also worried about not telling anyone about that. Although Paul worked as a corrections officer in a jail an hour out of town, he still frequented the area, and he still had anger issues from what she'd heard.

"Okay, spit it out. What are you not telling me?"

She locked gazes with Unc. "It's not a big deal. I shouldn't let it bother me."

"What is it?" He leaned forward and held her gaze. Unc had that look. A very hard, determined look that seemed to be able to tell if a person were lying or something. It must have to do with his law enforcement background.

"Well, yesterday, around lunchtime, I received a text message. I really don't think it's anything to worry about, but—"

"From Paul?" he asked, his voice changing to a deeper yet calmer tone. She locked gazes with him and saw the concern.

"Yes."

He released an annoyed sigh.

"What did the text message say?"

"'How are you? I miss you. Hope all is going well.'"

"You didn't reply, did you?"

"Of course not. I ignored the text."

"Did he text again?"

"No."

"Good. You let me know if he calls you, or if you see him when you're out. I don't trust that guy, for obvious reasons, but I also don't trust his friends. He had help getting those charges dropped."

"I had to drop the charges, Unc. Uncle Brian was killed in the robbery, I was so depressed and felt abandoned and weak."

"I was there for you to lean on. You should have shared your concerns with me."

"Unc, I'm sorry. It was just easier to let the assault charges stick than to pursue the entire other charge, drag me through a trial, testifying in front of strangers and everything else that would come from that. I wasn't in the right frame of mind to fight that battle. Besides, like the lawyer said, we were dating, proving rape would be almost impossible even with the assault charges, and the recorded injuries I sustained. I couldn't handle it physically or emotionally. Not when mourning Uncle Brian. Why the hell are we having this conversation again, anyway?" she asked, feeling frustrated.

"Because Paul contacted you and I know what he did to you that night. He got away with all of it. He even got to keep his job."

"Well, family ties with politics helps a lot, now doesn't it? Us lowly servants to the system need to pay our dues and work our asses off. Ya know, the old-fashioned way."

He shook his head and stared at her.

"Becoming cynical now, too?"

"You must be rubbing off on me."

"I'm not cynical. I just believe that justice should be served. That little asshole will get his one day. He can't keep out of trouble."

"I'm sure you're right, and I really don't care either way. Well, I'd better get a move on it. I need to head home, shower, and change and then meet up with the girls."

"You be careful. Make sure they lock up before they leave that place of yours. Remember when I stopped by a few weeks ago and Donella's window was unlocked. With her room in the front of the house by the garage, anyone could break in and take her. None of you would hear a thing."

"I know. I got on her for that and so did Moira and Jessie. I guess I'll see you next week. Hopefully we can do lunch."

"I expect that to happen. Family is important, friends come and go." He stood up and pulled her into a hug.

"Thanks, Unc. Talk to you soon."

She exited the bar waving a good-bye to some of the regulars as well as to Ray. As she got into her car, she pulled out her cell phone to check it before she started driving. When she saw the multiple texts from her friends, she smiled, but then she saw the one from Paul.

You can't ignore me. What we had was special. I'll see you soon.

The tears filled her eyes, and that feeling of uncertainty and fear gripped her chest. Was he messing with her to scare her on purpose, or did he really think that she would forgive him for assaulting her both physically and sexually?

Her therapist's words popped into her head. "He's only as strong as you allow him to be. You're different now. You're a fighter, a survivor."

Maybe taking Moira up on her offer to attend those private self-defense clinics should become a priority?

Chapter 2

Ellie was locking up and checking all the windows and doors in their house before they left for the night.

They were dressed pretty sexy, except for Ellie. On their insistence she wore a dress even though she wanted to wear pants. She wore dresses and skirts every day for work. But Moira, Donella, and Jessie were fashion gurus. They knew what the latest styles were down to their Jimmy Choo shoes. Tonight in particular, Donella was sporting a black designer dress that hugged her curves, and she sure did have curves, the trim lining the bottom of the dress where the material bounced against her upper thighs was hot pink. She wore black stilettos that matched with hot pink along the bottoms, and on the strap.

Moira wore her signature green and black. The color matched her eyes and brought out the natural Irish glow of her skin. Then there was Jessie. A Texan through and through, she wore a pretty tight red dress with sequins along her bust line that accentuated her deep cleavage. Wearing her custom-made, designer red-sequined cowgirl boots with high heels made her shapely calves and thighs look amazing.

"Damn, Ellie, that dress fits you like a glove. How come you've never worn it before?" Jessie asked her as she joined her in the living room.

"I forgot about it. But Donella was in my closet and just so happened to place it on the bed as a hint."

"Well, she did good. You have got the perfect figure, for a petite little thing," Jessie stated, giving her the once-over with a smile.

"Plus she has the boobs to hold up that strapless dress. Never mind the muscular legs to wear those Louis Vuitton heels. Those are so sexy with the strands of beads hanging in the back over the high heel. The colors match the sequins along the trim at the top of the dress," Moira stated.

"Told you. Now are we ready to go have a great time or what?" Donella asked.

"Maybe I should take my own car. I mean if you're planning an all-nighter, I have to meet that client tomorrow afternoon, early evening," Ellie stated.

"Nonsense. We're going there together. Now let's get moving."

* * * *

Ellie was laughing so hard at the story Sam was telling her and Moira. A Texas Ranger, retired from the military, the man had such an ability to tell a story he should be onstage. He was very attractive, and Moira was definitely interested in him and his three brothers. It just didn't seem fair for other women that one woman could snag three or even four sexy men at a time. But being in Casper's where a lot of retired military men hung out, there were ménage relationships all around them. It actually gave Ellie a sense of calmness and safety. Maybe because she figured most of the men were taken, and others that seemed to be single weren't acting like jerks.

"You are so funny. Isn't he, Ellie?" Moira asked her as Moira grabbed on to Sam's arm and hugged it.

Sam's eyes lit up, and anyone with any clue could see the desire in them. Moira just might get her wish after all.

Ellie took a sip from her drink and looked around the bar. She could see Donella doing some shots with a few guys, and Jessie was talking to another set of people by the jukebox.

As Ellie glanced to the right, she spotted one man limping slightly as he walked toward her direction. She wasn't certain why, but instantly her senses kicked in. He was tall, at least six foot two, with shoulder-length blond hair that looked untamed and wild just like the expression on his face. He appeared angry, determined, almost mysterious.

She felt the nudge against her arm, and Moira whispered, "That's Hunter Lawson. He's a friend of my brother Caprio. He and his brothers, the three guys coming in behind him, are big shots. They don't usually hang out here. They're probably here for the party in the back."

Ellie immediately turned away as Hunter locked gazes with her and seemed pissed off.

As she thought about what Moira told her, she thought about Moira's brother, Caprio. He was a really nice guy, hard around the edges but totally gorgeous. He'd served in the military up until two years ago when he was injured and lost his leg in combat. Her brother had a hard time dealing with his injury but pulled through last year with the help of some of the guys around the town who were also retired military. Ellie had even attended some sports competitions Caprio and other amputees were part of. In fact, there was a running event next week they were going to attend to see if Caprio made it to the sections championship. If he did, he would head to the state championship next.

"Hey, Justice!" Sam yelled out over Ellie's shoulder, waving someone over.

Before Ellie turned, she sensed the large figure behind her. On instinct she moved to the left and bumped into someone.

"Hey." The abrupt tone had her standing still and frozen in place.

To the right was the huge man with shoulder-length blond hair and deep green eyes, and next to him, the one she'd bumped into, was just as fierce looking. He had wavy blond hair, scruff on his face, and very blue eyes.

"I'm sorry." She quickly turned back toward Moira. Moira eyed over both men with interest and then smiled.

"Moira, Ellie, meet some good friends of mine. This is Justice, his brother Hunter, and over there are their other brothers Seno and Mace. They're on their way over now."

Both men looked at her and Moira, and then Justice and Hunter stared at Ellie. She could sense their eyes on her even as she turned to look away. There was a strange sense of awareness. Where she had met other men, even tonight, and shared a few casual glances, none had made her body react or her skin feel their presence. Out of a combination of anxiety, and a bit of fear, she remained looking toward Sam and Moira.

"Hey, looks like you've got your own little party going on over here. Can we join?" Donella asked, sounding tipsy as she bumped into the guy, Hunter.

She must have hit him hard or maybe took out his knee or something because he cursed and looked as if he would fall. Ellie grabbed him around the waist, stopping him, as he used his other arm to brace the bar. It all happened so quickly. The feel of solid steel beneath her hand, the tattoos and Marine Corp symbol on his upper arm, the odd feel of his leg against her leg made her think he wore something over his leg and under the jeans. It was so weird. She must have looked at him oddly, because he snapped.

"What?"

She shook her head. But instantly she thought that maybe he was an amputee, too. Moira did say that Hunter was friends with Caprio. She suddenly felt as if she'd insulted him somehow but didn't know why or even how she could have. She didn't have to fret over it long because Donella made a complete ass of herself.

"Hey, just because you're klutzy doesn't mean you can yell at my friend," Donella stated.

"Donella, don't. It was just an accident. I think maybe you should slow down on the drinks."

"I think you ladies shouldn't be arguing over that brother when there are three others to choose from."

They all turned toward a blonde woman they didn't recognize at all. But Moira did, as she shot daggers with her eyes at the woman. She looked like a stuck-up model with her flowing golden locks, two-sizes-too-small glittering blue dress, and diamonds galore. She licked her lips as she eyed over Justice and the other two men but not Hunter.

Hunter got the evil look women give men who've done them wrong. And on top of that, the woman rubbed Sam's shoulder and arm until Sam stepped away from her, drawing Moira into an embrace. It was a sure show of public display to say Sam wasn't interested in this woman.

"Take a walk, Ray Anne," Hunter stated. Ellie looked at him, noticing the way he stood so authoritative and tough. Any fool should recognize a look like Hunter's.

The woman stared at Hunter and then at Ellie and Donella. Ellie was holding Donella's fruity-smelling drink in her hand, which she had taken away from her as she wondered what the heck was happening here.

Moira stepped forward, giving Ray Ann the evil eye. "I don't recall anyone inviting you to this conversation. No one is interested in what you have to say," Moira stated toward Ray Anne.

Ray Ann looked right at Ellie. "Take some advice from a woman who knows, you don't want to waste your time with Hunter, not unless you're into being a Good Samaritan."

"Cool it, Ray Ann," Justice said, raising his voice. For some reason Ellie didn't like this woman one bit at all. Also, one look at the four brothers, and she could see the hatred, especially from Hunter.

"Take a walk," Sam told Ray Ann. When he took Moira's arm to lead her away to probably avoid a situation, Ray Ann shot nasty daggers at Hunter and then toward Donella.

"You're a pretty little thing. He'll eat you alive, one legged or not," Ray Ann said with such venom.

Moira pulled from Sam's embrace.

"You better take a hike. He's a marine. You don't deserve to even be in this place."

Ray Ann flicked her fingers at Moira as Sam pulled her back.

Ellie thought that if Hunter did have only one good leg that it was pretty damn despicable for Ray Anne to make such a comment. Moira had a soft spot for any injured soldier, never mind one who reminded her of Caprio. Ellie was feeling pretty protective herself right now as she looked at Hunter and saw both the rage and the sadness. It touched her heart.

"What's the matter, Hunter, going after little mice you can boss around to make yourself feel more like a man?"

"That's enough. Get out of here, Ray Ann," another man stated. By the similar features and green eyes of Hunter, Ellie thought he was a brother. She also realized that the blonde woman was calling her a mouse.

"Who are you calling a mouse?" Ellie asked, feeling her own annoyance with this stupid woman get under her skin.

"Ignore her," Hunter whispered from behind her. Ellie looked at him again, and couldn't help but care.

The blonde looked her over, her eyes zeroing in on her breasts, which were at least three sizes bigger than the blonde's.

"You better like it on top. Soldier boy only has one leg, so you'll have to do all the work in bed."

The shock and disgust that filled Ellie's heart was instant, and being one to sometimes react without really thinking things through, she tossed the contents of her glass right at Ray Anne's chest.

Ray Ann gasped as Sam released her arm to move out of the way.

"Why, you little bitch. How dare you?" she screeched, drawing more attention to them.

Ellie stepped forward and pointed at Ray Ann. "No. How dare you? You don't belong in here. You belong outside with the rest of the trash," Ellie told her and the bar erupted in cheers, taunting Ray Ann and booing her out of the place.

Ellie was so embarrassed, but also so fired up, that she was shaking.

"Ellie that was awesome. I've never seen you so pissed off and ready to fight. You may not even need those self-defense classes we talked about," Moira stated.

"Self-defense classes?" Justice asked, as Hunter turned away from them and sat down on the barstool.

"Yes, she needs them, or at least she does if a fight was to get physical," Moira added.

Justice and his two other brothers stared at her, looking her over. She nibbled her bottom lip and held Justice's gaze.

"A beautiful woman like you shouldn't have to get into any physical confrontations," Justice told her.

"Sam, I hope you were going to tell these lovely ladies about our private self-defense training groups Justice and I do."

"Those aren't for civilians, Mace," Hunter barked from behind her.

"We've done special favors before. For friends, that is," Mace said and then winked.

"By the way, I'm Mace and this is Seno." Mace introduced him and his other brother.

She smiled. "Ellie, and nice to meet you."

She noticed how Donella, Sam, and Moira began to slink away, and the Lawson brothers moved in around her.

"I really can't stand that woman. It's good to know that a girly drink to her outfit could get rid of her so quickly," Mace said as he moved next to her.

"I can't believe that woman could say such things. We were involved in our own conversation. It's so immature," she replied.

Seno stood next to Mace watching her.

"You held yourself well. So what's this about self-defense training?" he asked.

She lowered her eyes. "It's Moira's idea. Her brother Caprio knows some guy or something that does these classes in one of the training facilities by the racetrack. We might check it out this week."

"Oh, I think I know who that is," Mace said and then winked at Seno and Hunter. But Hunter immediately looked away when she glanced at him. She wondered if somehow, despite her standing up for him, if she also insulted him. More importantly, why did she even care when she didn't know him or his brothers?

Mace continued to talk with Justice about some upcoming hand-to-hand combat games sponsored by the local YMCA. She had the opportunity to absorb their similarities as brothers as well as their differences. Seno was the only brother that had dark hair. The others were blond. They were all very tall, at least six feet, and well built. Justice and Mace had blue eyes where Seno and Hunter had green eyes.

Before long she found herself engaged in conversation about Casper's and about what they did for a living as the crowd around them grew louder and bigger. There was a roar of excitement behind her, and when she turned, she saw some guys getting rowdy and picking one of their friends up in the air. They began to sing "Happy Birthday," and the crowd of people moved causing her to step right in between Hunter and Seno. The moment she felt the hand on her hip and the protective semicircle around her, she paused in awe. The four brothers surrounded her, being sure to keep her safe from the rowdy guys around.

It had suddenly become so loud from the singing that she squinted her eyes, and covered her ears with her hands turning toward the bar.

When she did, she locked gazes with Hunter who stared at her.

"I didn't need your help," he told her. She uncovered her ears and stared up into his eyes. Behind her someone bumped into Seno and she pressed closer to Hunter. She grabbed onto his arms to steady herself.

"I'm sure you didn't, but she was obnoxious. I dislike obnoxious people." He must have thought she was referring to him. His hold tightened.

"You think I'm obnoxious?" he asked, and the feel of his hands on her hips aroused her. Nothing seemed to matter but the lost, hurt look in his eyes, and the sensation that pulled at her heart.

"I don't know you, Hunter. Although first impression is that you have an attitude."

"Yeah, well my first impression of you is a woman who knows how to throw a drink to hit her target."

She stared at him uncertain if he were flirting, or what?

"How about I buy you a new drink?"

"Hmmm. I don't accept drinks from strange men I just met."

He raised his eyebrows at her. "But you will defend them on intimate bedroom information publicly announced to a crowd of other strangers?"

She looked him over. He was handsome. He was rugged looking, but it was that look in his eyes, the fear, the sadness, that she recognized as familiar.

"I guess I was relying on instincts. You know, my gut."

He gently used his thumbs to massage the sides of her hips as Seno pressed against her back, shocking her.

"What is your gut telling you now?"

Her mind erupted into some mighty naughty thoughts, especially as she looked to the right. There were Justice and Mace, close enough to kiss.

"I think it's telling me I should run while I can."

Justice smiled and then reached over and caressed her chin, making her look at him.

"When this night just got a hell of a lot more interesting? I don't think so. Let us buy you a drink. That way we can work on getting your number and making plans," he said confidently.

She chuckled. "Nice try. Has that actually worked for you in the past?"

Seno caressed her back. "Every time," he whispered.

She stepped from their hold and smoothed out her dress.

"Well, it was very nice meeting you. Glad you have a whole scheme and plan to hook up with some unknowing female. "

She started to leave, not missing the disappointed expressions on Hunter's and Seno's faces.

Justice took her hand. "Hey, don't leave. Stay and talk. We didn't mean to come on too strong."

She smiled. "I need to find my friends. Besides, it would never work out."

"Why not?" Mace asked.

"I don't date." She walked away, and as she did, she couldn't help to feel disappointed. She liked them. That was a first, liking more than one guy at once, and in turn it had her looking back over her shoulder. She nearly lost her footing as she saw all four men staring at her walking away. She felt herself shaking, concerned about how she looked in the dress, and wondering why she allowed Donella to talk her into wearing this dress. With fears from her past, and her intense need to remain in control and not affected in any way by a man, she straightened her shoulders and prayed for confidence. She was used to hiding her fears, even from her friend. So she did what any single, attractive woman in this type of situation should do. She walked as sexy and casual as possible and hoped that she didn't just miss out on one hell of an opportunity. A disappointed feeling consumed her. *When will the fear I have lessen? Why can't I just move on, and take a chance?*

* * * *

"Wow, she is gorgeous. A petite little thing, too," Seno said and then took a sip of his beer.

"Tough, too. Sure didn't fall for your little play, Justice. That's a first," Mace stated and they chuckled.

"I guess I came on too strong." He looked around to where she had disappeared.

"I think you did," Hunter said with an attitude.

Seno looked at Hunter. He definitely was attracted to Ellie. Hell, they all were. But his attitude was where their issues started.

"I liked her, too. I think we need to find out more about her," Mace suggested.

"That will be simple. We'll ask Sam. He'll know. Seems like he and his brothers may be interested in Ellie's friend. It was Moira, right?" Justice asked.

"Yes," Seno replied.

"Well then, to finding out more about Ellie." He raised his mug of beer.

"To hoping she doesn't throw a drink in one of our faces," Seno said, and they laughed and then clanked their mugs together before taking sips.

Seno smiled as he looked around the bar and spotted Ellie talking with her friends. He couldn't help but feel some bit of hope that they met Ellie together tonight, and they all liked her. If fate sent her their way again, he would personally make certain to leave a lasting impression.

A short time later, Seno noticed a guy, Hartford, was standing mighty close to Ellie. He watched his hand move around the chair she stood by and then go to her waist. Ellie side stepped away, but Hartford moved closer again.

"What are you staring at looking so pissed about?" Justice asked.

"In about two seconds, I'm going to go over there and give that guy a piece of my mind. His hand keeps moving closer and closer to her ass. What the hell?"

Seno saw Hartford touch Ellie's hair as he placed his hand on her waist again. He was about to go over there, but his brothers stopped him.

"Look, she's pushing his hand away and saying something to him. She's not interested in him." Mace added.

Seno continued to watch her, feeling possessive, even though he had no right to be.

"We're going to get to know her. I say, if our paths cross again, we ask her out on a date."

"Well duh, of course we will. It's not every day you meet a woman that can grab the attention of four brothers, especially when one of the brothers is adamant about meeting a woman." Justice said.

"She's special. I just know she is."

Chapter 3

"Morning," Donella said as she walked into Ellie's bedroom.

Ellie smiled as she looked at her poor hungover friend.

"It's afternoon, Donella," Ellie replied. She stood in only a strapless bra and panties as she stared at three dresses lying on the bed.

"Yeah, well, I don't even care what time it is. It's Saturday, my day off."

"Not mine. I can't figure out what outfit to wear."

Donella placed her mug down on the dresser and stood next to Ellie to stare at the dresses.

"Well, you said the business date is at Tratorra's right?"

Ellie nodded.

"Is this business guy hot?"

"What does that matter? It's business."

"Did you land the deal already, or is it determined by the outcome of this meeting?"

"Well, I'm pretty sure we snagged it. I mean he did want to show me more ideas for the designs and artwork."

"So it's not a done deal. Go for the power play, the red number, with those black and red Jimmy Choos. The length is conservative for the red dress but the shoes say powerful, sexy, a woman of class and sophistication. You're petite so you don't want to come across as a pushover."

"I don't know. I think red is too sexy. The black one is more conservative and the red one really presses my breasts together causing a deeper cleavage."

"That's what you want, sexy. You said this guy is loaded, the deal isn't sealed, so hit him with the big guns, and who knows, maybe he can be a little business fling when the job is complete."

"I'm not interested in him. He's not even my type."

"Girl, who is your type? You turned down four sexy brothers last night that most, if not *all*, the single ladies, me included, were drooling over."

"I did not have a chance with them."

"Keep lying to yourself. You're gorgeous, you're intelligent, classy and well built, and self-maintained. Those are characteristics of a woman who is not meant to be single."

"Donella, please. We've been over this before. I'm not ready. Besides, you forget, I choose to be single."

Ellie picked up the red dress and slipped it on. She had to readjust her boobs into the top, as Donella zipped up the back.

"Baby, you've been saying that for so long. It's more than time to move on. You can't stay scared forever. Don't you want to find someone who could treat you right, and perhaps love you for who you are?"

Ellie lowered her eyes. "I do, but I am scared. There's nothing I can do about it but wait. When I'm ready, I'll know it."

"I can understand the fear you still have. What Paul did to you was horrific, and I know you're still trying to deal with that. I just don't want you thinking that there's something wrong with you. It was all him. He wasn't right. You're beautiful, you're smart and classy, and you can have your choice of a man. You just need to take a chance. If you get that feeling inside that you're attractive, then just go with it. Flirt a little, feel the guy out, and when you feel comfortable, accept a date. It's a start," Donella said with a smile. She really was a great friend.

"You make it sound so easy. I'm just not sure if I can handle everything that goes along with a date. Mostly being alone with a man. I just don't think I'm ready, even though the desire to have someone, to be cared for or even loved is something I know I want one day."

Donella squeezed her shoulders. "You're more than ready now. Just take that leap of fate. I'm sure you'll know when the time is right. Oh, and there are always double dates, group dates, or casual gatherings where we can accompany you so you feel more confident." She winked and smiled.

Ellie pulled from her hold. "I can't. I won't. There's too much to fear, too much to have to face."

"God, Ellie. Paul really fucked up your head. I thought that therapist you were seeing told you it was time to move on and give dating a shot."

"She said when I was ready. Don't you understand that I'm the one who has to go through everything? The questioning of whether or not my instincts are right about a man. Not knowing what could set a man off and make him attack. Not knowing what it is I'm looking for in the right man or whether I'm asking too much or too little. It's just overwhelming, and I haven't even gotten into the intimacy aspect yet. I can't. It's too upsetting. How can I trust a man when I can't even trust myself because I'm so scared?"

Donella took her hand and held her gaze.

"You're right, I don't understand. I didn't go through what you did. But you survived. You've moved on with your life and have put Paul behind you. I'm just saying that maybe if you just try dating or even becoming friends with a guy first, it could work out. You know, ease your way into the intimacy of dating?"

"I don't know. Maybe making friends first might work."

Donella smiled and then looked Ellie over. "Or maybe just going right for the sex might solve the whole fear factor. You look incredible."

Ellie blushed and then stepped into the high heel shoes. She did look good. She needed to land this deal and get that bonus she had coming. She'd deal with the making-friends-first thing another time.

"Okay, I need to go. I'll see you tonight."

"Maybe you won't," Donella teased, raising her eyebrows up and down in a silly way. Ellie chuckled.

"Later."

* * * *

Detective Justice Lawson was looking over the crime scene photos from the latest victim. The case had a few similarities to three other cases in the area, but this woman was last seen at a very exclusive party. His partner, Vin Elloy, Sam's brother was talking to someone on the cell phone. He said thank you and then got off the phone.

"It's confirmed that the last person she was with was someone working for a guy named Renaldo Sentinel. He was hosting the party the other night."

"What's the guy's name that this woman was with?"

Vin looked down at his notes. "Luke Phillips. He's this guy's personal assistant and security man. I have someone tracking him down now."

"Good. Did you hear from the lab about the hair samples found on the body?"

"Not yet. Hopefully by later today."

"Okay, then let's go over these files again and see if we can establish a credible link. We'll need to meet with the commander before we head out. If we have a serial killer on our hands, the sooner we identify that, the more man power we can get to find him or her and stop them."

"You got it. Let's do it."

* * * *

Ellie pulled up to the valet parking and was escorted to the front entrance. Before she even made it to the reception area of the grand restaurant and hotel, a woman with red hair and a huge smiled greeted her.

"Miss Morrison?"

Ellie nodded her head.

"I'm Alecia. Mr. Sentinel is expecting you. He asked that I escort you through the cigar lounge so you can begin to get an understanding of the artwork on display."

"Of course. Thank you." Ellie pulled her iPad out of her bag and walked along the corridor. She took pictures of what had first caught her eyes and where she felt things were missing. From the entryway to the reception to the cigar lounge and now a back private room.

"Miss Morrison, so nice to see you again." Luke Phillips greeted her by gently taking her hand, lifting the top to his lips, and kissing it.

She smiled. "Nice to see you, too, Mr. Phillips."

"Please, call me Luke. Renaldo will be here momentarily. He is taking an important phone call."

Just then the door opened and Renaldo appeared. He paused a moment taking in the sight of her and then smiled.

"You are a vision in red, Ellie. You look stunning." He greeted her with a kiss to her cheek and a gentle arm around her waist. He stared down into her eyes and held her gaze, pulling her snugly against him.

"I've waited weeks to get a better view at your gorgeous green eyes. I hope the tour was informative," he whispered, letting his hand glide over her lower back to nearly her ass as he released her and offered her a chair at the dining table to the right of them.

She swallowed hard, feeling a bit of an attraction toward the man. But who wouldn't be attracted to a multimillionaire with dark mesmerizing eyes, a debonair personality, and exquisite taste?

"Thank you, you're very kind. The tour was informative as you intended."

He waved toward the server standing by, a man dressed as a formal waiter, with a sharp white linen towel draped over his arm. He approached the table and poured two glasses of wine.

"I hope you don't mind that I took the liberty of ordering a few of my favorite dishes for you to experience. I'm planning on keeping them in the new menu for my latest chain of restaurants."

"Of course. I'm sure I will be very happy with your choices."

"Are you now? Is it because you trust my judgment and taste or are you simply appeasing me?" he asked with an heir of arrogance that had her defensive radar rising.

"Of course not. You may not realize this, Renaldo, but I have very opinionated tastes. It will be amusing to see if you and I share some similar likes."

"Amusing? I would prefer stimulating," he countered, holding her gaze and looking her cleavage over with interest. She felt the heat hit her body and wondered how this business dinner meeting was turning into something else. She lowered her eyes and adjusted her napkin on her lap.

"I'm so sorry. I didn't mean to make you feel uncomfortable. I enjoy conversing with you. You're a realist, but you have the quality of shyness I'm truly attracted to."

The waiter arrived, thank goodness, with some appetizers. Oysters on the half shell, shrimp scampi, and some stuffed mushrooms, her favorite.

"Oooh, I love stuffed mushrooms," she stated, inhaling the wonderful scents and aromas.

"One of my favorite as well. Go on, let's enjoy this." She placed a mushroom on her plate as Renaldo began to talk about his plans for the restaurants, the décor, and keeping similar aspects of Tratorra's.

"Might I suggest a very different entryway, and foyer, perhaps even an area where guests wait for the table or can enjoy a cocktail before or after dinner while being enthralled with some of your more outlandish art."

"Outlandish?" he questioned.

She smiled. "Sorry, I do not mean to insult. Everyone is entitled to their taste in art. However, I would really like to know why you display a million-dollar piece by the reception area? It seems outlandish to me."

He chuckled. "So the tour was informative?"

"Would you like to go over my findings and ideas to see if I'm the right person for this project?"

He smiled at her, then took a sip of his wine while holding her gaze over the rim of his glass. "I'm hopeful that you fit this project quite well, so you and I can work side by side."

She smiled as she pulled out her iPad and began to go over what she had seen and some ideas of how to improve the initial ambiance of the restaurant when guests first entered. She went as far as showing him some pictures of general ideas and fine art that wasn't nearly as costly as the paintings he displayed without a care for their price tag or their effect on the patrons.

"You can truly awe your guests by establishing a gallery for their viewing as they wait. If done in the right way, it could bring in even more patrons and give you the opportunity to enhance other rooms in the restaurant."

"What do you mean?" he asked, moving closer to view the pictures.

Before long she was suggesting theme rooms so that he could get the feel and look he wanted in his choices of the various Venetian arts he insisted on using throughout the place.

When she felt his hand smooth over her knee under the table, she looked up at him.

He held her gaze. "I knew you were right for the job. This is going to be great. How quickly can you start?"

She was shocked at his fast-forward personality.

She closed up the iPad and clasped her hands on top of the table.

"Well, Mr. Sentinel, we'll need to finalize the contracts with my boss."

"Already done. I spoke with him ten minutes before you arrived."

She went to speak and was speechless.

He moved his arm over her chair behind her back and inched closer.

"I'm looking forward to working with you, and getting to know you, Ellie. Now let's enjoy dinner and then we can work out a schedule for the coming few months."

He eased away from her, her heart pounding, her hands instantly clammy now that she could breathe again. The man was a force, and very demanding. But he was also sexy and attractive, with oodles of appeal. She smiled, feeling pretty damn happy for getting this job, and hoped she could pull off what he wanted.

"Oh, and please call me Renaldo." He covered her hand with his and gave it a squeeze as he winked.

The rest of their time together flowed smoothly, and Ellie couldn't help but to think of her conversation with Donella today. Could she take a chance and try dating again? Was Renaldo right for her, or would he be a mistake? Or, could she be so brazen as to entertain a sexual fling, no strings attached, in order to help her get over the fear Paul put into her? She wondered and then thought about Paul and his text messages. How could she move on when the man who'd destroyed her life, gave her all the fear and trust issues she had, still held power over her. Even if it was the power of fear?

* * * *

"Did you guys have a good time last night?" Vin asked Justice as they drove out of the police department and headed to interview Luke Phillips.

"Aside from that bitch Ray Anne saying that shit about Hunter, yeah, it was an all right night."

"Would have been better if you guys hooked up with Sam's friend, Ellie. She's gorgeous."

Justice glanced at Vin and then back toward the road.

"She seemed nice."

Vin chuckled. "Nice, my ass. The four of you couldn't keep your eyes off of her. I thought Seno was going to start a fight with that guy, what's his name? Oh, Hartford, something Hartford. That guy has got the touch with the ladies, but your little spitfire wasn't biting."

Justice smiled to himself. Seno was going to go over there and rip the guy's arm off. Every time Hartford moved his hand over her waist and then grazed her ass, Seno wasn't the only one seeing red. The woman had a great ass. It stuck out, and her dress accentuated the roundness of it. She may be petite, but she had sexy curves. She wasn't skin and bones, nor was she what he considered chubby. She was perfect.

"She turned him down, too."

"She sure did. Maybe she's seeing someone."

"Sam said she isn't. After you basically had Sam give Moira the third degree."

"So we're interested but Ellie said she doesn't date. Maybe the whole ménage thing intimidates her?"

"Well, it sure as shit doesn't intimidate Moira."

Justice looked at Vin and saw the odd expression. "What's up? I thought you guys were all interested in dating Moira?"

"Oh, we are, it's just that she's a bit young, inexperienced, and we've been down that road before. It wasn't pretty."

"Oh yeah, with Tara. She was too young, and wanted to party all the time."

"Exactly. But she was something else in bed."

Justice chuckled. "That right there probably added to how it went all wrong."

"What the hell do you mean?"

"You thought more about how the sex was with her instead of the strong feelings, the bond and connection that sets a ménage apart from a damn orgy."

Vin chuckled. "You're right. But it wasn't our fault. The sex was the best, but as far as bonding or having a connection, it wasn't there at all."

"Do you think it could be there with Moira?"

Vin looked out the window. "I'm not sure. We don't want to rush into it, so being friends right now, flirting a bit, is fine. If it turns into something more, then we'll just have to wait and see. So when are you going to try and snag Ellie's attention and get her to give you guys a chance?"

Justice smiled. "The next time my brothers or I see her, we'll be sure to start getting her to be more comfortable with us. I guess the friends and flirting thing will be first for the four of us, too."

"This may call for some sneaky planning."

"What do you mean?"

"A party at our place after the races next Saturday. That's sure to provide a more relaxing setting."

"You think Ellie will go to the race and then your party?"

"I'll talk to Moira. She said that Ellie and her are attending the races. Ellie had an uncle who was retired from the police department but was killed over a year and a half ago. It was in New Castle, a few towns over."

"Oh yeah, the robbery at the convenience store on Smith. Two crooks died, the retired cop, and the clerk, too."

"Yes. It was tragic."

They pulled into the parking lot and decided to park the car instead of using the valet.

"Hey, you can't park there," some kid in a vest told them. Vin flashed his badge.

"We won't be long." The kid nodded his head and headed toward another car that just approached.

As they entered the place, Justice was surprised by the upscale décor and fancy chandeliers.

"The food smells good," Vin stated as he rubbed his belly. Justice smiled as they approached the front reception area.

"We're looking for Mr. Luke Phillips. We were told he was dining here today," Justice stated toward the woman.

"Is he expecting you? I don't have another party joining him."

"No. We'd like to speak with him please." Vin flashed his badge and the woman's eyes widened and then she smiled at Vin.

Her cheeks took on a rosy shade of pink and she nodded her head. "Of course, Detective."

She picked up the phone and whispered into the receiver.

Vin and Justice stood by the waiting area, absorbing the decorations. Some of the items were eye catching, but nothing grabbed his attention like the brunette in red walking down the hallway escorted by two men in designer suits.

As they came closer, he felt his heart race and his eyes widen at the sight of Ellie walking between the two men. Was she with them? Did she belong to them? Both men paused and one guy—tall, dark hair, very upscale—took her hand and kissed the top of it.

She smiled and nodded her head, and then he placed his hand on her waist, leaned forward, and kissed her cheek. He couldn't be a boyfriend. If he were, he would have kissed her on the mouth. He wanted to feel relief, but instead he felt more on edge, especially when she turned to shake the other man's hand and he leaned forward and kissed her cheek. As she started heading toward them, the two men watched her, eyeing over her backside until she locked gazes with him.

The woman from the front desk pointed toward Vin and Justice and both men looked. Their expressions changed and so did Justice's. Ellie was hanging out with a man who they needed to question about a murder.

* * * *

Ellie felt her belly quiver after having such a nice lunch with Renaldo. He was so suave and very good at flirting, that she found herself flirting back and wondering where it may lead. After Luke received a phone call as the lunch was ending, they parted and now she was heading home to ponder over her reaction to the charismatic man. After they both kissed her good-bye, she headed toward the main entrance and nearly lost her footing as she locked gazes with a fierce-looking Justice Lawson. He was dressed in suit pants, dress shirt, jacket, and tie, and was staring at her along with Sam's brother, Vin.

They looked at her and then back toward Luke and Renaldo, and for some strange reason she felt guilty.

"Hey, what are you two doing here?" she asked.

Justice looked her over and she felt her nipples harden as her breath caught in her throat. That was a first for her.

"I could ask you the same thing. You know those two?" he asked with an attitude.

"I'll give you a minute. I'd better go introduce myself," Vin said and then winked at Ellie before walking away.

"What's going on?" she asked.

"Business." He looked at the cleavage of her dress and then down into her eyes. Even with the Jimmy Choos on, he still towered over her.

"Business? You're a detective. What type of business would you have with Renaldo and Luke?"

"You know them well?" he asked, giving her an expression as he grazed over her body again. His question was laced with hidden meaning she was out of practice of identifying.

"No. Business," she added with an attitude.

"I may need to talk with you. Stick around if you can." He walked away and toward his partner, Luke and Renaldo not giving her an opportunity to respond. She wondered why she had a feeling that this situation wasn't good at all.

* * * *

Vin did not like either man's attitude nor did Justice once he joined the conversation. Vin could tell that Justice was fired up seeing Ellie dressed in a sexy red dress and knowing one of the two men they were questioning. He hoped that Justice kept his cool.

"Listen, we understand that there were a lot of people at that party, but the woman in question was found murdered. We need to speak with anyone who was seen with her the other night. Multiple people named you," Justice stated toward Luke.

"I remember her. She was a regular."

"A regular?" Vin asked.

"Detective Elloy, is it? She was a woman who frequented many upscale parties in search of landing a wealthy man. All I can tell you from conversations we've had in the past was that she was working her way through school and trying to establish a modeling career to boot," Luke told them.

"Are you saying that she was prostituting herself?" Justice asked but then kept his eye on Renaldo who seemed pompous and disrespectful.

Luke chuckled and raised his hands palms forward. "A lot of women become obsessed with money, and like I said, landing a wealthy man. She's one of many. I'm sorry that I can't be of more assistance."

"Sure you are," Justice added, giving Luke the dirtiest look Vin had ever seen him give someone.

"What is that supposed to mean?" Luke asked.

"Nothing. Here's my card. If you think of anything else, please don't hesitate to call me. It could help us find her killer," Vin stated as Luke took the car and stared at Justice.

"Prostitute or not, murder is a crime, and the killer will be caught and brought to justice. I'm certain that the two of you upstanding citizens would like to be part of solving that crime," Justice said. He smiled and winked and then walked away. Vin followed.

"Holy shit, partner, I don't think I have ever seen you give the looks you were giving that Sentinel guy."

Justice remained silent as they headed out of the place.

"Was it how much of a pompous asshole he was being along with Phillips, or the fact that he had his hands on your woman?" Vin asked.

Justice gave him a look, but as they headed toward the valet, they both saw Ellie getting into her car.

Justice hurried over as Vin walked to get their car.

* * * *

Ellie didn't know why she felt guilty and nervous or why she told the valet four times to get someone else's car so she could wait for Justice. A series of thoughts went through her head. Were Luke and Renaldo involved in some sort of illegal activity? Was Justice angry with her for being there with them? But none of it seemed to affect her more than thoughts of whether or not Justice found her attractive or was jealous seeing her with two other men. Not that anything was going on, but by his and Vin's expression, it sure did seem to look that way.

She couldn't wait any longer without seeming like a woman with a crush on the sexy detective. Even his gun and badge on his waist aroused her. How silly. The fact that Justice was even involved in law enforcement should make her weary and stay clear. Paul was a correctional officer. He carried a gun. Hell, he used it to assault her that night. She felt the tears sting her eyes, and she swallowed hard as she got into her car.

"Ellie."

She heard Justice's voice as she closed the door. She pressed the automatic button to roll down the window. He leaned on the doorframe and looked into her eyes and then over the cleavage of her dress.

"Yes?"

"Can you follow us out of here? It's important.

She nodded and he stared at her a moment as if he wanted to say something and then didn't. He walked away and she pulled out onto the main road and drove slowly until Vin passed her. She followed them about a mile or so toward another shopping center and into the back parking lot.

It was warm out. About eighty degrees as she exited the car.

Vin and Luke walked over. Vin smiled and then looked at Justice who seemed pissed off.

"How do you know Luke Phillips and Renaldo Sentinel?"

"Business."

"What kind of business?" he asked, looking her over. His expression seemed guarded, yet his eyes showed his upset.

"You seem agitated at me. I don't understand why. Did I do something wrong?"

"You tell me. We're investigating the murder of a young woman. Phillips was one of the last people to be seen with her. He said she was a high-priced prostitute trying to land a wealthy man."

Once again she shot from the hip, and was immediately offended.

"And what? You think I'm a high-class hooker who just finished servicing Phillips and Renaldo?" She raised her voice on the last syllable and Vin jumped in.

"No. Of course not. That's not what my partner is insinuating, honey." Vin placed his hand on Ellie's shoulder and she stared up into Vin's eyes.

"Well, what is your partner insinuating then?" She looked toward Justice, who ran his hand through his wavy blond hair. His blue eyes looked fierce.

"What kind of business are you doing with them?" Vin asked.

She explained about her company, about the designing, and about the new project as she reached into her car and pulled out her iPad. She showed Vin the pictures.

"You have to work with those men for how long?" Justice asked, sounding pissed off.

"I don't know. However long it takes. Why? Do you think they're involved with this murder? You think they killed this woman?" she asked, suddenly feeling very scared and nervous. She crossed her arms in front of her chest and looked from Vin to Justice.

Justice stepped forward and placed his hand on her left hip. He stared down into her eyes. "I'm sorry that I got angry with you. I'm just concerned. We don't know how involved these two men are in this. It's not your concern. As of right now, they're not suspects, we were just questioning them as a lead in the case."

He reached toward her face and cupped her cheek as Vin walked back toward his car. She looked toward him but Justice used his thumb to caress her chin, and she looked back up toward him, uncrossing her arms.

"When I saw you in there with them, it pissed me off. My brothers and I were kind of hoping to get to know you better."

"Justice, I told you that I don't date."

"Why is that?"

She looked down and he used his thumb to draw her attention back toward him. She stared at his handsome face, his firm lips and couldn't help but feel the attraction.

"I can't explain it, but I just don't jump into dating men."

He stared at her and then smiled, moving his hand further behind her and against her lower back. He drew her against his chest and she placed her palms against his chest.

"You look gorgeous in red. The color suits you."

"Thank you."

He stared at her and he was so intimidating, so charismatic that she faltered under his perusal.

"Perhaps we can take things slowly, and maybe become friends first? Then, if the attraction is shared, we can take the next step. What do you say?"

"Justice, I don't know." She started to continue to deny his idea but then he raised one eyebrow up at her in such a sexy way, she found herself smiling.

"Okay. But no promises. I'm really not ready to date again."

"Ah, sounds like a bad experience may have had something to do with this crazy idea of never dating again."

"Maybe, but it has nothing to do with being crazy and everything to do with being cautious."

He squinted his eyes at her and she hoped he didn't push for more details.

"Okay. Now, I want you to be careful around Phillips and Sentinel. If they ask if you know Vin and I, say yes, that we're friends. It's a small world. But don't ask them anything about the woman. This is a police investigation, understand?" His tone, so firm and authoritative, was sexy just like the rest of him.

"Yes, Detective Lawson."

He released her, but not before letting his hand slide over the top of her ass. She couldn't help but wonder if that were his way of compensating for the fact that Renaldo did the same thing and that had pissed Justice off.

She waved to Vin who waved back, and then she got into her car and headed toward home, hoping that her two bosses weren't murderers, and that Justice wasn't anything like Paul.

Chapter 4

It was Wednesday afternoon and Ellie stopped by one of the local delis to grab a salad with grilled chicken. She was starving, after her meeting at the art gallery went on two hours past schedule. Some of these art fanatics could be so temperamental. However, money could influence even the stingiest of sellers, and Renaldo had money. He wanted one particular painting that went for five hundred thousand dollars. She had to admit that the people at the gallery were difficult to work with. When her boss asked her to step in and negotiate the deal after another employee failed, she hesitated, feeling that it wasn't part of her job. But if she realized anything working with her boss, he was a man of action and expected results.

As she opened the door and stepped in line, she glanced around the deli, debating about sitting or taking her order to go. That was when she locked gazes with Mace Lawson.

He waved at her and she waved back just as the cashier asked to help her. She ordered her salad and a homemade sweet tea to go. After getting her meal and paying for it, she started to head out when the door opened and Seno walked in.

His eyes widened in surprise and he looked authentically happy to see her.

"Hey, Ellie, how are you?" he asked.

"Over here!" they heard someone call out. Seno took her arm, and they headed toward the table where Mace was. Mace stood up and greeted her with a kiss to her cheek, and damn she was feeling some seriously crazy things. She was instantly attracted to both men, and had that same feeling of desire she had for Justice.

"Late lunch?" Seno asked as he held out a chair for her.

"Yes. I really should head back to the office. My meeting went too long."

"Oh, stay and have lunch with us. We were both stuck working past lunchtime, too," Mace stated.

He gave her a smile and she shrugged her shoulders as she started opening up her to-go container. As she reached for her plasticware, one of the cashiers brought over Seno's and Mace's hero sandwiches.

"Hello, Mace. It's nice to see you again." She licked her lower lip and gave him a sexy smile.

Ellie widened her eyes and focused on her salad.

"How's your boyfriend Duke?" Mace replied, taking his seat and staring at the woman. She shrugged her shoulders and then looked at Ellie.

"That outfit is gorgeous."

"Thank you," Ellie replied.

"I agree, you look beautiful," Mace stated, staring at her, and the cashier walked away.

She stuck her fork into a piece of chicken without letting her eyes leave Mace's ocean blue ones.

"Glad to have helped you out of that situation," she whispered.

"What situation would that be?" he asked, as he unwrapped his hero.

"The young cashier with a crush on the older, attractive male and his similarly strikingly handsome brother."

"You find me attractive?" Mace asked, holding her gaze.

"And me strikingly handsome?" Seno asked.

She shook her head and laughed then began to eat. Her phone started ringing, and glancing at the caller ID, she saw that it was Renaldo.

She looked around to see if she could get up to take a call but the place was crowded.

"I'm sorry, I need to answer this." She placed the phone to her ear. "Hello?"

"Hey, gorgeous, how did the gallery situation pan out?" Renaldo asked. He was speaking loudly and she was certain that both Seno and Mace could hear him.

"Everything is set."

"Fantastic. I owe you for taking care of this so professionally and smoothly. Dinner tonight, at Redalphos's?"

She pulled her bottom lip between her teeth.

"Dinner isn't necessary, Renaldo."

"Oh please, I insist. It's been a successful first week, only Wednesday and you've accomplished so much. I can have a car pick you up at your place or at work."

"I'm running kind of late. As a matter of fact, I'm just having lunch, and then I have a lot to accomplish for the builders by Friday. So dinner really can't happen tonight. I probably won't even be able to leave the office until late."

"I'm disappointed but impressed with your commitment. We'll make plans for Friday or the weekend. I need to go. Thank you again."

"You're welcome."

She pulled the phone away and placed it onto the table. Both Mace and Seno were staring at her.

"Who's Renaldo?" Mace asked. She thought for sure that Justice would mention him but then why would he? She'd made it clear to Justice that she wouldn't date him or his brothers right now. Besides that, it was a police investigation and she was certain they had confidentiality clauses.

"That's someone I work with."

"Declining dinner at Redalpho's? I hear that place serves a mean chicken Parmesan," Seno stated.

"It is a nice place, but I really have a lot to do at work. I'll probably be there late."

"You should be careful. Is there security that can walk you out to your car?"

"No, but there is security inside the building and they have cameras on the outside. I'll try to park closer to the building as precaution."

"Good. So how about those self-defense classes? Are you, Moira, and your other roommates going to sign up for some?" Mace asked.

"To be honest, I don't think I'll have much downtime to do any. Even on nights that I'm not late coming home, it may be closer to eight o'clock and the sessions take place earlier."

"We can help you. Seno and I, and Hunter, too. We have access to the gym by the track and indoor dome," Mace told her.

"That's okay. You don't need to do that."

"Hey, if it means spending more time with you, and letting you get to know us, I'm in," Seno added.

"Hey, seriously. Think about it. We can start next week if this week is so crazy," Mace told her.

"Okay. I'll think about it. Thank you."

Her phone started buzzing and she glanced at it. "Work. I guess I should just take this back to the office. It was nice seeing you both again. Tell Hunter and Justice that I said hello." She wasn't sure why she said it, and as she did, her cheeks felt warm and her heart light. She smiled at Mace and Seno as they stood, each gave her a kiss on the cheek good-bye, and then she left.

It was crazy, but she felt very comfortable with them, too. If she could just slightly peel down the wall enough to entertain this attraction, maybe it would be okay. Maybe she would be okay, instead of feeling so timid and unsure. She walked to her car, as her cell phone went off again. Work, work, work. She wouldn't have time for a personal life right now even if she had one.

* * * *

"So you saw her at the deli, and had lunch with her? What did she have to say?" Justice asked Seno and Mace as Hunter and he sat in the living room.

"Who did you say called her?" Justice asked. When they told him about the guy Renaldo, he cursed. He couldn't help it. He didn't care for him or that Phillips guy one bit. They were rich assholes, who could care less about the dead girl.

"What? Do you know the guy?" Mace asked. Justice explained how they had met and about the case.

"And you're letting her work for this guy and his partner? What if they try something with her or hurt her?" Hunter asked.

"I don't think this guy had anything to do with the murder. He has an alibi for the time of death and her disappearance. It doesn't conflict with the coroner's report of the time of death and circumstances."

"Great, and she's working late tonight and there's no security outside in the parking lot," Mace told them.

He explained about their conversation.

"One of us should go over there and be sure she's okay," Seno suggested.

"We can't do that. We're not her boyfriends, yet. It could scare her. She had a bad experience, I think, and that's why she's resistant to dating. I think she wants to be friends first and ease into a relationship." Justice told them about the short conversation.

"So someone hurt her and she's distrustful?" Hunter asked.

"Seems that way. She's really sweet though. I think she's a good person but fears a repeat bad relationship. The only way to be sure is to get to know her and talk."

"I agree."

"Well, so does Sam. He has a plan," Justice said and then explained it to his brothers.

"Party at Sam's and his brothers' sounds like an awesome idea. There's plenty to do there, including that swimming pool," Seno stated.

She's really going to the race Saturday?" Hunter asked.

"That's what Moira told Sam," Justice replied.

Justice looked at Hunter, and he could see the concerned expression on his face.

"What's going on in that head of yours, bro?"

"Nothing," Hunter replied and then stood up, stretching his leg. He wasn't wearing a prosthetic device as he reached for the crutches he kept around and started to move toward the kitchen. Hunter was in great physical condition. He was always working out, competing in races, and even Spartan events. He was one of a few amputees that could finish one of those intense races. His brother didn't let his loss of half his leg from the knee down stand in the way of anything he wanted. However, since meeting Ellie, Hunter seemed discouraged.

"You know she likes you, don't you, Hunter?" Seno asked before Justice could.

Hunter looked back toward them and stared at all three of them.

"I don't need sympathy," he replied.

"Sympathy? You seriously think Ellie feels sympathetic toward you and nothing more? She hardly batted an eye at your leg," Mace stated.

"She did more than bat her eye. She stood up for me as if I were disabled and unable to fight my own fight. She also turned us down as a whole because I'm not whole. It's the same ole, same ole. I'm sick and tired of it. You guys move on and be happy. It's all I really want in this world anymore."

"Absolutely not. I can't believe this shit is coming out of your mouth, Hunter. You, the man who doesn't back down from anything, is telling me that you're giving up on our dream? You're no longer interested in sharing one woman and completing this family? Ellie is the first woman to come along who we all are attracted to and are willing to take our time getting to know," Justice said to Hunter.

"That's because she's sweet, and our buddies are good friends with her roommate. If there were no other connections, then the three of you would have seduced her into bed that night at Casper's."

"Oh man, you are so wrong. Entirely way off. I thought you had more self-confidence than any man I've ever met. Now here you are feeling sorry for yourself, for the fact that you have half a leg despite all you've overcome and accomplished? Hell, Hunter, we all have our heavy baggage from the service. Just because the three of us have our limbs and all our parts doesn't mean we don't have scars and bad memories. I think Ellie is the one. Call me fucking crazy, but I haven't even been able to look at another chick since meeting Ellie. And I have access to a lot of sexy, hot chicks willing to rub and tug with a snap from my fingers," Seno stated, sounding angry as he stood up and began to pace.

"I think we need to calm down here. It's obvious that Ellie affects us all. It's not a bad thing. Now, Hunter, just keep an open mind and let's see if this leads anywhere," Justice stated.

"That's easy for you three to say and have such hopes for. I've been with a few women since losing my leg. I see that look in their eyes as they avoid looking down, or that expression of pity. It tears right through my heart. None of you get that. After Ray Anne, I just don't think I have it in me to receive a look like that from Ellie or any other woman the three of you think might be the 'one.' Sorry, but it's just the way I feel."

Hunter walked out of the room, leaving Justice, Seno, and Mace alone to ponder over his words.

"I didn't realize how badly he'd been feeling. He puts on such a show, his tough guy, soldier face," Seno whispered.

"Fucking Ray Ann fucked with his head. We should have seen that, and should have intervened," Justice added.

"We couldn't do that and you know it. He was getting some, and he seemed happy. We all let it go despite the signs that Ray Ann was a manipulating bitch," Mace stated.

"Well, Ellie put her in her place. I don't think Ray Ann will ever walk into Casper's again," Justice said and chuckled.

"That's a good thing so she won't be able to take advantage of some other soldier, or a man like Hunter who just wants to be accepted for who he is and not pitied. What if we're wrong, Justice? What if Ellie is just being kind and sweet because she feels sorry for Hunter? If we get close to her and want to take her to our bed, will she make us choose between her or Hunter?" Seno asked.

Justice held his brother's serious expression with one of his own.

"I sure as hell hope not. Hunter is our brother. If the woman we want can't accept Hunter for who he is, then that woman is not the right woman for us and our family."

Chapter 5

"What do you mean he texted you, Ellie? How many times? Why didn't you call me immediately the first time he did?" Unc asked as she spoke into the phone and packed her bag. She threw in her bathing suit, towel, toiletries, and a change of clothes and whatever she thought she might need for Sam's party.

She looked at Moira who could hear Unc's loud voice through the phone.

"I'm telling you now, Unc. It's been bothering me, even though his texts don't really sound threatening, just innocent."

"Innocent, my ass. That man is a monster who should still be behind bars. I'm going to call Detective Ramirez."

"But there isn't a reason to panic. He can't hurt me, Unc."

"Bullshit he can't hurt you. I was there at the hospital after he attacked you. I was with you during your recovery along with the girls. Moira's there. I'm sure she recalls your nightmares and screaming down the house."

Ellie swallowed hard as Moira squeezed her shoulder and smiled.

"I know. I don't want anything bad to happen to them and I don't know Paul's state of mind right now either."

"Exactly, honey. That's why I'm going to call Ramirez. If he wants to stop by to see you, I can meet him at your house."

"Oh, I'm heading out with the girls. We have an event to go to and a party."

Unc was silent a moment and she worried that he was so concerned.

"Are you sure you want to? I mean I'm not trying to make you nervous but I don't trust Paul and his capabilities. He still wants you. He thinks he owns you."

"I know that. We always take precautions. Besides, we'll be at Sam's place. He's having a party. You know him and his brothers. There'll be a lot of police around."

"Well you be sure to lock up your windows and doors before you leave. Set that alarm, too."

"I will, Unc. If Ramirez wants to talk to me, he can call my cell."

"All right. Have fun, baby girl."

She smiled. "I will. Bye."

She disconnected the call and released a sigh.

Moira sat down next to her on the bed. "He's worried just like I am."

"I don't want to overthink this and ponder over Paul's actions. Yet, I feel on the defensive, and like I should be better prepared for anything. I hate this feeling. I'm tired of being scared, Moira. I'm tired of not feeling safe, of worrying about whether or not Paul might show up, or even try to hurt me again. I'm sick of not being able to trust another man, and overanalyzing every single guy I meet. I've been throwing all my energy into my work so that I don't ponder so much about the what-ifs. I just want to feel safe and loved. Is it too much to ask?"

She wiped the tear from her eye before it fell as Moira pulled her into a hug.

"I don't know what to say to help ease your mind. All I can tell you is that being cautious is not a bad thing. You should trust your gut instincts, as well as your heart. You're a good person who sees beyond the materialistic, and even the cover or façade of a person. Paul took advantage of that, but you're smarter now. You know the signs of control, danger, and that sensation in your gut that says it's all wrong. There is a guy out there who will find you and love you for who you are. He will make you feel protected and loved. Hell, there may be more than just one. Maybe four." Moira winked and Ellie shook her head.

"I don't know what I'm going to do about that situation. I'm too fearful. I don't even know how I'll react if a guy kisses me. I could feel panicked, trapped, I don't even know."

"Well you won't know until the time is right, and when that kiss or kisses happen, you'll get your answer. It may be rough at first and you may get that panicked feeling, but just slow it down, pull back, and if the right man is kissing you, he'll understand. He won't push. He won't force himself on you. He'll slow things down with compassion and care. Then you'll know, Ellie."

Ellie smiled as Donella entered the bedroom. "Are you two ready? The race is going to start in an hour and seats will be filling up fast."

"We're coming," Moira stated.

"Hey, you're not wearing the red bathing suit today, are you? Because I'm wearing my red one and your breasts look better than mine in the red bikini you have, Ellie."

Ellie laughed. "No, I'm wearing the emerald green one, thanks to Moira accidentally throwing my red and black bikinis in the dirty laundry."

Donella chuckled and Ellie looked from her to Moira, who shrugged her shoulders.

"Why do I get the feeling that you two planned this? Where's Jessie. She'll fess up."

"I'll fess up on what?" Jessie asked, entering the room carrying her bag and wearing a slim-fitting black sundress.

"Nothing, nothing. We just made certain that Ellie wore her sexiest bikini today. She looks fabulous in green and it brings out the emerald color in her eyes. Besides, that sexy sundress you're wearing matches perfectly." Donella, Moira, and Jessie chuckled as they headed out of the room. It seemed to Ellie that her friends were trying to play matchmakers. So why was she feeling anxious and nervous, and well, excited about going to this race? She pictured Hunter in her mind and then Justice, Seno, and Mace. Four sexy, seemingly nice men who were drop-dead gorgeous and very interested in getting to know her better. What better way to ease into feeling comfortable with the opposite sex than to attend a sporting event and then a party?

Hopefully, it wouldn't turn into a disaster.

* * * *

He walked into the restaurant over an hour ago, his mind juggling a thousand things. He knew that the shithead was up to no good. But he had a plan. One that would take out this asshole the way he should have been taken out years ago. His vengeance had led to a compulsion, an obsession, and need to kill. No one would miss this asshole when he took him out. Just like they didn't miss that whore. She'd served her purpose well. Only temporarily, but she did well. She was pretty, just like this one.

He licked his lips and prepared to play his role. He had an agenda. His obsession and desire for revenge were eating away at his patience. He wanted his ultimate prize. He wanted to prove his commitment, and he wanted to make sure that justice was served. But he needed to be careful. Being a man of many disguises and personalities, he could pull this off. This one was perfect. She also just had sex with his number-two target. *Let's see how this plays out.*

He approached her carefully, being sure to keep his back toward the small surveillance camera near the bar. As he placed his hand on her hip, he sat down and casually ordered two drinks.

She looked at him, brown hair flowing, makeup perfect despite her recent roll in the hay with dickhead number two, and he smiled.

"I spotted you from across the room. A woman of class and sophistication. Sit with me for a spell, and I promise to make this the most memorable night of your life."

He pulled out his wad of cash, the hundred dollar bills covered the tip, but there was nothing but singles in between. This stupid bitch would only see the hundreds. The first step in drawing in his prey, before he pounced.

She ran her hand over his shoulder. He piqued at her breasts in the two-sizes-too-small dress she wore. Not exactly as large up top as he liked, but she would do. Not only to trap his other prey, but to satisfy that need, that obsession inside of him.

"My name is Tiffany. And you are?" she asked, rubbing her thigh against his leg as she took the seat next to him, nearly on his lap.

He lowered his face to her neck.

"Let's just say, I'm the man who's going to blow your mind."

* * * *

"There she is. They're making their way to the bleachers." Justice pointed toward Ellie, Jessie, Moira, and Donella as they squeezed through the crowd. He watched her, and saw three guys watching her, too. They called out her name.

"Who the hell is that?" Seno asked as they started heading toward the women. Mace was holding seats for them, along with Sam and his brothers.

"I don't know, but if his hand goes any lower, it will be over her ass. What the fuck is up with guys hugging her and planting their hands on her ass?" Seno asked as he and Justice made their way closer.

"Like we wouldn't do the same thing?" Justice asked, trudging forward and saying "excuse me" as he made his way through the crowd of people.

"At this point, I'd call the day a success if I could just hold her in my arms, even if just for a hug hello." Justice felt the same way as Seno.

* * * *

Seno watched Ellie's expression change to one of concern when the third guy pulled her into an embrace. She stiffened up, and seemed to put her hands against his chest in a defensive manner. Justice must have picked up on it, too, as he pressed right between the three guys.

"Ellie, ladies, there you are. Come on, we saved you seats down lower," Justice said. Seno winked at Ellie, who smiled wide.

"Hi," she said and totally didn't introduce him to the three men, or even acknowledge them any further. Nor did Moira, Donella, and Jessie who seemed upset to say the least.

As Justice took Ellie's hand to lead her down the stairs, Seno took in the sight of her. She looked gorgeous with her snug-fitting green sundress and strappy heeled sandals. Justice wrapped an arm around her waist and laid his hand possessively over her lower back and near her ass. Seno chuckled. His brother just couldn't resist. She was that appealing.

"Is Hunter nervous?" Moira asked him and Donella.

"If he is, he's not letting on. I think once he gets through the first race and can place in the finals he'll be good," Seno told them.

As Donella and Jessie walked ahead of them, Seno spoke to Moira.

"Who were those three guys talking with Ellie back there? None of you seemed thrilled to see them."

Moira rolled her eyes. "They're friends with an old acquaintance of Ellie's."

"Acquaintance?" he asked, raising one eyebrow at her.

"Her ex's cousins. Although the three of them are very interested in Ellie for themselves. No need to worry though, Ellie blows them off every time they approach her, call, or text her. She's not interested."

"And her ex? Is he around here, too?" he asked, glancing around them.

She paused and looked toward Ellie, her expression changing. She seemed nervous. He stopped her from walking.

"Moira, what is it? Is he around here? Is there need for concern?"

She swallowed hard and placed her hand on Seno's arm. "It's not my place to say anything about her ex. I like you and your brothers. Please take things slow. If you push her, or come across too strongly, she'll run. She's been through hell, a living nightmare, and the last thing she needs, or will accept right now, is any show of dominance and control."

Donella called her name and Moira smiled and then headed toward her seat. Seno glanced at Justice who took a seat next to Ellie. Their brother, Mace, was kissing her cheek hello and smiling.

Seno felt his chest tighten. It seemed their little spitfire had a painful past of her own. Could he and his brothers be patient with her as Moira suggested, or would their natural, dominant personalities scare her away?

He looked at Justice, who saw his concerned expression. "Everything okay?" he asked.

"Later. We'll talk later," he whispered as the announcer began the opening ceremonies.

* * * *

Ellie became excited the moment she had seen Seno and Justice. It was great timing to boot, considering that Paul's cousins spotted her and took the opportunity to hug her hello, caress their hands over her ass, and whisper how hot she looked. Those guys had no limitations. They knew what their cousin had done to her, and even afterward, when they stopped by to be supportive, they were already flirting and indicating that they were interested in her and would treat her the way a woman should be treated. Such jerks.

The sight of Justice and Seno totally, rudely interrupting the chance meeting, was appreciated, even if they didn't know what they were doing. Justice and Seno were way bigger than those men and they looked damn good. Justice and Seno wore blue jeans and tight T-shirts that showed off their muscular bodies. Both shirts had law enforcement logos on them in support of their department, and the team that Hunter was running for. She saw Hunter's matching shirt as well as Mace's. As Justice walked her down the stairs, taking her hand in a possessive manner, she felt that tingling awareness and acceptance to the feel of his large hand encasing her small one. But what shocked her most, and had her pulling her hand away, was the deep feeling of protectiveness, as well as physical attraction to him. She shared that same feeling when Seno kissed her hello, and now, when Mace placed a hand against her cheek and told her how beautiful she looked before he kissed her cheek.

She spotted Hunter standing near the track. He wasn't the only amputee running in the race. There were four of them and the other thirty or so were regular guys, or at least guys with both legs. She took in the sight of the metal leg, and thin silver arc that was in place of his leg and foot. Mace whispered next to her ear. He told her about the prototype, and about the special prosthetic devices that were available to men and women in the military who lost a limb while serving. There were plenty of others around them, and a sense of pride, respect, and also compassion overtook her mind. These men and women were no different than any other men or women who served. They were now dealing with their injuries the best way they could.

She looked around the crowd and saw families supporting their mothers, fathers, or spouses, and one little girl who jumped up into her father's arms caught her attention. The man, a soldier who Justice waved to, had only one arm and one leg. Yet he held his daughter up against his chest, a huge smile on his face and hers as he introduced her to other runners. She watched Hunter, standing alone, looking very serious, and she was certain if she were closer that she would see the sadness in those eyes as well.

As everyone stood for the national anthem, she watched in awe as everything stopped. No one moved or spoke as a young teenage girl sang the anthem in front of the very large crowd of people.

When it was over, everyone cheered, the excitement of the race beginning momentarily.

"Damn, I can't believe Theo is here. That fucking guy is fast," Mace stated toward Justice and Seno.

"I know. Hunter saw him. I hope he doesn't let that guy in his head. It's tough enough that no one with a handicap has ever won this race," Mace added.

"What?" she asked, shocked at the news. She figured with all the different people racing that it could go either way.

"No amputee has ever won this particular race before. If he wins this, it will be a great achievement for Hunter," Justice told her as he took her hand, squeezed it, and held her gaze.

She looked back toward Hunter, who just so happened to glance up into the crowd at them.

"He'll do it. He's got that look in his eyes," she whispered, never letting her gaze leave Hunter's until Hunter turned away and began to warm up, jumping high in the air in place, working out his legs.

"What look is that?" Mace asked, leaning closer to her and placing his hand on her knee.

"The eye of the tiger," she said, just as the announcer asked all runners to take their positions.

* * * *

Hunter was shaking. He had trained for this race for over a year's time. Last season he failed to even come into the semifinals because his mind wasn't focused. He thought when he broke things off with Ray Anne months ago that once again he would lose his focus, but surprisingly he hadn't. Instead, as he looked up into the crowd and saw his brothers, his friends, and Ellie and her friends, he felt motivated. He wanted to prove to everyone, including himself, that he wasn't an invalid, a pity case, but instead the same strong, determined fighter he always had been despite the missing leg.

As he prepared to race, he focused on what he needed to do. As the gun fired he took off, knowing that he had worked so hard to succeed.

* * * *

They were all caught up in the action and excitement of the race. Five miles, twenty times around the large track and it was torture to watch. She felt just as nervous as Justice, Seno, and Mace when they watched runners slowing down, losing their positions. When Hunter and Theo were neck and neck, and Hunter was the last amputee with a chance at winning, never mind placing in the race, the crowds grew louder. By the final two laps they were all standing, chanting, yelling Hunter's name.

As they hit the final lap, Hunter's silver leg, like some bionic instrument that allowed men like him, heroes, to continue to strive for success in life, pounded against the red racetrack. Theo was falling slightly back as they rounded the last turn and Hunter started sprinting. Justice, Mace, and Seno were yelling his name, chanting him on, and so were their friends and others around them.

She knew in that moment that it would come down to the man who was most hungry for the win. The one destined to take first place and stand on that podium of champions and know that he was the best of the best. A warrior, a fighter, who never gave up.

As Hunter's chest hit the red ribbon stretched out across the track, they all screamed and cheered his name and Hunter bent down, catching his breath but also covered his eyes with his hand, bringing tears to Ellie's.

He was an amazing man.

They all made their way down to the racetrack as the runners took their positions on the podium. She took pictures with her cell phone as he received his medal and a huge trophy. She watched in awe as so many people came up to congratulate Hunter and then it was their turn.

As she approached, watching his brothers hug him and then Sam and his friends, she smiled.

"That was amazing, Hunter. You are amazing." He nodded his head at her as they held one another's gaze a moment while everyone around them talked and laughed.

"Let's keep this celebration going. Our place ASAP," Sam said and the guys all cheered.

Ellie stood next to Mace as she watched Hunter pull off his drenched T-shirt. He was covered with muscles and tattoos grabbing not only her full attention, but also the attention of a number of young women who watched him and whistled.

She felt that instant sting of jealousy, just as Mace placed his hand on her hip and whispered down low next to her ear. His warm breath tickled her neck, as his lips touched her skin.

"Don't worry, Ellie. We only have eyes for you." He gave her hip a squeeze and then took her hand and walked hand in hand with her as the others headed out toward the parking lot.

Chapter 6

Hunter watched Ellie talking with Sam's brother, Link. He was the CEO of a large advertising firm outside of Dallas. He was laughing at something she said, and then he reached over and clutched her elbow. He recognized the feeling that hit his gut. He knew himself well. The possessiveness he had when he found something or in this case, someone, who interested him. That jealous feeling that some other guy would impress her more, make her see his imperfections. He was compelled to demand for her to pay attention to him and see him for more than what was right before her eyes. An amputee and a cripple.

"What's that look for?" Seno asked as he approached Hunter.

Hunter glanced at him and then nodded his head toward Ellie and Link.

"They're getting along well. She's very likable," Seno stated.

"More than just well. He's touched her elbow or nudged her shoulder several times in a short period of time," Hunter replied.

"First of all, he's got his eye on Moira, just like his brothers Vin and Sam. Secondly, she's not biting on any invites from any men. I was talking to Moira in the stands at the races, after I saw three men approach Ellie and hug and kiss her." Hunter squinted his eyes at Seno, instantly feeling jealous again.

"Ellie didn't look too happy, and when Justice interrupted the conversation, Ellie and her friends were more than eager to get away from the three men. Then when I asked Moira about them, she said the three men were cousins of Ellie's ex."

"What?"

"Yeah, and get this. The three cousins are interested in Ellie, but she isn't. She keeps blowing them off. I tried to find out more about the ex, but basically Moira wasn't budging. She hinted that Ellie went through some nightmarish experience and she asked that we all take our time with Ellie and to not be overly commanding. Seems something bad happened to Ellie."

"Hey, you two, are you going to join in the party or what?" Sam asked, approaching them from behind.

"Sure are. This is great. Thank you for inviting us," Hunter stated.

"Inviting you? Hell, this party is for you. I knew that you would kick that Green Beret's ass," Sam said and then smiled. Hunter and Seno chuckled.

Hunter watched Ellie excuse herself from her conversation with Link and then head inside, answering a call on the way.

* * * *

"Hello, Detective Ramirez. How are you?"

"The question is, how are you? Unc called and said that Paul has been texting you. How long?"

She took a deep breath and released it as she walked toward the side of the cabana and away from the music and people.

She took in the tropical décor and the large sitting area and couch. Her back was toward the door as she spoke to the detective.

"Do you know where he is? I mean is he local again? Because I saw his cousins today, and they were aggressive in their comments."

They talked about what he knew and how Paul was reinstated into the corrections job he had before the assault.

"Are you kidding me? How could they hire him back? After what he did to me? I was in the hospital for weeks."

He went on about him serving part of his time, about the community service Paul did, and about presenting his case to the board about his counseling for anger management.

"He has a lot of friends, Ellie."

"Well that's great, Detective Ramirez, now isn't it? So I have to worry about these text messages, and the fear I've had to deal with for over a year that was beginning to lessen has just skyrocketed again because of this conversation. Goddamn it. It isn't fair."

She heard a sound and turned to see Hunter standing there leaning against the door frame. He looked so pissed off. She could hardly focus on what the detective was telling her. He said something about getting an order of protection.

"An order of protection cannot be obtained because of text messages. Besides, I've been there and done that, and look where I wound up. I'll just keep doing what I've been doing. Watching my back, looking over my shoulder, and living my life. Thanks for nothing, Detective. I suppose I'll call you if something more takes place." She ended the call and then collapsed down onto the bench right behind her. She covered her face with her hands and growled low. She was so frustrated.

Plus now Hunter heard part of her conversation. This was all she needed.

"Are you okay?" he asked as he took the seat next to her. She shook her head.

He reached over and moved her hair from her face. She turned to look up toward him. The man was so damn sexy and attractive, but she couldn't take the chance her mind was begging her to take.

"Want to talk about it?" he asked.

"Absolutely not. I'm frustrated, angry, disillusioned, and mostly fucking scared. I can't believe that this is happening. A year. A Goddamn year and just when I'm feeling back in control and stronger mentally, this happens?"

She crossed her legs and leaned back against the bench seat. Hunter didn't say a word. He just seemed to watch her. She tried closing her eyes and breathing through her anger and her outburst. It seemed to work and she opened her eyes and released a long sigh.

"I'm sorry. I totally didn't mean to just blurt all that out, or to have you overhear my conversation."

"I wasn't eavesdropping. I saw you head this way and wanted to talk to you. Then I heard you mention a detective, an order of protection, and something about you being in the hospital for weeks. I was concerned."

Her eyes widened when he said hospital for weeks. She didn't want to tell him about Paul and about the assault. She didn't want any of this crap to be part of a potential relationship. But now, after talking with Ramirez, her hope of there being any possible relationship just diminished. She couldn't get involved with the Lawson brothers. Not if Paul was going to pursue her again.

She stood up, but Hunter grabbed her hand. She turned toward him and he pulled her closer and between his thighs. Surprisingly she wasn't turned off by the prosthetic device he wore from his knee down. The masculinity of his muscular thighs, and his sexy chest she had gotten a glimpse of uncovered, aroused her.

"Don't run away from me, from us," he whispered.

She licked her lower lip and he pulled her onto his upper thigh.

He placed one arm around her waist to hold her in place on his lap and the other hand he placed on her thigh just barely below the hem of her dress. She wondered what it would feel like to be caressed by such large, capable hands.

"God knows we all have secrets, or experiences we'd like to keep hidden, but, baby, you look more scared than angry, and that just isn't sitting right with me."

"Hunter, it's not your concern."

He gave her hip a squeeze. "You are my concern, and my brothers'. If this situation you're in is what's keeping you from being with us, then I think it's something you, Seno, Mace, Justice, and I need to discuss."

She shook her head and turned further into him to face him.

"Please, Hunter, just leave it alone. It's not a situation, yet. It may never become one. It's just something that happened to me." She lowered her eyes. She felt his palm caress back and forth over her thigh and then under the material.

She held his gaze, his expression serious, but also the sadness in his green eyes so apparent. It tugged at her heart.

He moved his hand from her thigh, she felt the loss of his touch, but held his gaze. He placed his hand against her cheek, and she absorbed the feel of his masculinity and the scent of his cologne, fresh soap and enticing to her senses.

"A beautiful woman like you shouldn't be afraid." They stared at one another and she glanced at his lips as he glanced at hers. She wondered if he would kiss her and she hoped that he would.

His lips softly touched her own and they both closed their eyes.

Ellie was lost in his hold, his kiss, and the connection she felt to Hunter. He was different right now then the other times she had been around him. He wasn't fierce, confrontational, and angry. Instead he was calm, empathetic, sexy, and macho in every sense of the words. He used his tongue to explore her mouth and then moved his hand back against her thigh, pulling her harder against his chest.

She kissed him back, battling for control and then indulging in his taste, his commanding kiss, and the power and safety she felt in his arms.

When he moved his hand under her dress and up the back of her thigh, she felt her heart racing and her body tighten up. She was incredibly aroused as she explored his hair with her hand running her fingers through the blond, shoulder-length locks. They were moaning, or maybe it was just her as she felt embarrassed by her reaction to Hunter. She started pulling back and he pulled her tighter before gently releasing her lips and kissing along her jaw and then her neck. She was trying to catch her breath, feeling overwhelmed at her reaction to him.

Hunter didn't move his hand from under her dress and against her thigh nearly to her ass. Just a few inches and he could caress her ass cheek and probably make her come right here on his lap. She felt her cheeks warm and he smiled.

"Damn, I could kiss you for hours, Ellie."

She sat up and ran her fingers against her lips in an attempt to destroy any smudge marks.

"Oh God, we should probably head back to the party. They'll wonder where we are," she stated, preparing to move off his lap, but he held her in place.

She raised one eyebrow at him in question and he nodded toward the doorway.

There stood Mace. Crew cut blond hair, decked out in swim trunks and some T-shirt with what looked like John Wayne on it. It didn't fit his macho, tough-guy attitude at all. She pulled her lip between her teeth as he walked closer.

"What are you two up to?" he asked as he reached out and cupped her chin. She tilted her head up toward him, holding his gaze.

"Just talking," she replied, and he used his thumb to caress along her lips as if her lipstick were smudged.

"Just talking?" He raised one eyebrow up at her, as Hunter moved his hand up her spine, under her hair to the base of her neck. When his lips touched her bare shoulder she swallowed hard.

"Your lips look full and swollen, and your pupils slightly dilated. That could mean only one thing?"

"What's that?" She asked as he lowered his face toward her.

"I'd have to be sure before I can state with confidence the reason for your swollen lips and arousal in your eyes."

"Arousal?" she questioned just as Mace lowered his lips to hers and began kissing her.

* * * *

Mace was pleasantly surprised to walk in on Ellie and Hunter making out in the cabana. It was a relief and gave him hope that they had a chance to start something wonderful with her. But now, with his lips against hers, hearing her soft moans of pleasure as Hunter held her on his lap, he felt about ready to burst with desire. He felt that instant connection and desire. It felt right. Being here with Hunter and Ellie felt perfect.

He sensed her pulling back, and as to not overwhelm her he released her lips. He used his thumb to caress along them and smiled.

"You're delicious," he told her.

Slowly she stood up, with Hunter holding on to her hips from behind and standing along with her.

"I'm going to head back to the party."

"Everyone is either in the pool or the Jacuzzi," Mace told her.

"Then I guess I'll join them."

"We'll talk later, Ellie, okay," Hunter stated.

Her expression looked concerned but she gave a small smile and then headed out of the cabana.

Mace smiled at Hunter. "She's incredible. How the hell did this happen? The two of you in here?" he asked. When Hunter explained about what he overheard and what little he found out, Mace was pissed off.

"We need to talk to Seno and Justice. She could be in danger, and we can't just ignore this and what you overheard."

"I know, Mace, but I don't think she wants us or anyone else to know. She's scared, and demanding she tell us will only have her pulling away. That's not something I'm willing to chance. I care about her already."

Mace held Hunter's gaze feeling shocked at his profession of care for her and also pleased that Hunter wasn't running from it.

"Let's tell the others and see what they think. In the interim, let's enjoy the progress we've made today, and hope that it gets even better. I don't like the things that you overheard. Weeks in the hospital, an order of protection, text messages from someone, and speaking with a detective don't sit well with me at all. If she's in danger, I want to know about it."

"So do I. Let's see what Justice and Seno say."

* * * *

Ellie walked across the pool area some time later along with Donella. She explained to her about the phone call from Detective Ramirez and the latest news. Now even Donella was upset.

She could see Justice and Seno in the pool by the deep end talking to Sam, Vin, Mace, and Hunter. The moment she locked gazes with them and saw their expressions, she knew they were talking about her.

"Oh God, Donella. They're talking about me. I'm sure Hunter told them about the phone call."

"Honey, I don't think that's why they're staring. I'd say it has something to do with your sexy body, your belly piercing, and that sexy tattoo of yours that disappears under your tiny green bikini."

"Oh God. Maybe's it's your red bikini?"

"Nope. Don't let on to their gawking. Let's sit over there by the little end and just dip our feet in."

As Ellie sat down on the edge, the heat of the paving stone was burning her but as she reached down to splash water onto the side so she could sit.

"I'll grab a towel," Donella said as she walked over to the bags. But before she returned, Justice and Seno joined her, swimming through the water, holding their beer bottles in the air.

She sat with her hands on either side of her trying to act relaxed. But nothing about seeing Seno and Justice bare-chested made her relax. In fact, she could feel herself begin to drool and then she licked her lips.

"Wow, you look gorgeous in green," Seno told her as he eyed her body over, making every inch of her react as if he touched her.

Justice, on the other hand, eased into position beside her and leaned his back against the side of the pool, inches from her thigh.

"Here, this is for you. Link is making me one right now," Donella told Ellie as she passed her a frozen margarita.

"Oh, tell him I said thank you." She looked toward Link and he waved.

It was pretty hot outside and she could feel the sweat begin to move down her back.

"It's so hot," she stated.

"Come in the pool. It helps," Justice told her.

She placed the margarita down on the side and then slowly made her way into the pool.

They watched her swimming backward a few feet away from them as she cooled off when suddenly strong arms wrapped around her waist from behind. She gasped, and then turned to see Hunter. His thick, hard body pressed against her back and her ass as he swam her back over toward Justice and Seno. When he leaned against the side of the pool, he didn't release her, but instead kept his palm flat against her belly as if he had every right to hold her so intimately. Justice smiled and then took a slug of beer.

Seno handed her margarita and they started talking about starting a game of volleyball.

At one point Justice was watching her and kneeling in the little end of the pool. "Ellie, come here."

She looked at Hunter and felt his palm gently tap her belly before he released her. She swam toward Justice and his huge chest and big muscles. Pulling her into his arms, he stared down at the cleavage of her breasts and then back up toward her face. Her eyes looked over his tattoos, his bulging muscles, and slight dusting of hair across the center of his chest.

"You're just filled with surprises, aren't you, spitfire?"

"What do you mean?" she asked, and he tipped her backward so she lay flat in his arms and he lifted her so that she was floating on her back.

"Well let's see. First, this sexy body," he stated, and his brothers added their comments.

"How about that belly ring," Mace said and then reached over and gently wiggled it as he held her gaze.

"Or maybe this tattoo?" Justice said as he used his thumb to press along part of it and then he pressed under the material making her swat at his hand and then wiggle free.

They laughed, but Justice held her hand making her stay close by.

"I'm just teasing you, baby. You look incredible." He turned her in his arms so her back was pressed against his front. As they engaged in conversation about subjects she simply couldn't concentrate on while Justice pressed kisses to her neck, she started to feel overwhelmed. But then Seno told her about his special freelance job working as a criminal analysis for the Texas Rangers. Mace explained about his multiple jobs after retiring from the Marine Corp as a hand-to-hand combat instructor and coordinator for a nearby military training facility. His job sounded incredible and had her eyeing over his muscles along with the small scars here and there over his chest and a few by his sides. It appeared that he had some battle wounds, but before she could drool some more Seno teased him about his obsession with John Wayne.

"I love John Wayne. He was like the coolest cowboy ever."

"So that's why you were wearing that T-shirt," she said and smiled. She could understand the whole collector thing. She had a thing about collecting very expensive, limited edition shoes from famous designers.

"Yes, I have a lot of cool stuff autographed by him," Mace stated.

"Yeah, you should see the one room in the house that's filled with John Wayne memorabilia and also swords," Seno told her.

"Swords?"

"Yes, I collect specialty swords and knives." As he said "knives," she felt that bit of anxiety and fear grip her. Pulling from Justice's hold, she started to make an excuse to leave, but Justice pulled her back and wrapped his arm around her waist. The four men stared at her.

"He'd never hurt you. None of us would," he whispered against her neck. She felt her nipples harden as she saw Seno, Hunter, and Mace stare at her.

"I don't know what you mean," she whispered.

"Is that what happened to you? Did your ex pull out a knife on you?" Justice asked and she pulled from his hold.

"Don't. Don't talk to me about it. Don't ask me questions. Please, just leave it alone."

Mace took her hand and pulled her to him. "I'll get rid of all it. I don't need any of it," he told her so very seriously, and by the way his brothers explained about his collections, she knew that would be unfair. But she was deeply touched that he would say such a thing. She reached up and laid her hand against Mace's cheek.

"That's not necessary. I know what it's like to collect things. To have a love and appreciation for something specific like that."

"You do? What do you collect?" he asked, and she smiled, feeling better to have gotten away from a potential interrogation by these men.

"Very unique, limited edition, designer shoes."

He smiled.

"Oh God, that's not being a collector, that's being a woman," Hunter teased her. She gave him a mean expression.

"Not the kind I collect."

"You mean like Jimmy Choo, Christian Louboutin, Giuseppe Zanotti, or Givenchy?" Mace asked.

"Oh brother," Justice stated aloud as Seno laughed and Ellie smiled wide, holding on to his shoulders.

"How do you know about high-end women's shoes?"

"I know a lot of things, Ellie."

"I bet you do, Mace." She suddenly wasn't so freaked out about the sword and knife collection thing anymore. But considering the way the men were watching her with hunger in their eyes, she was relieved when the others joined them in the pool and started a volleyball game.

* * * *

As evening came they, were all having a wonderful time. They even talked about entering a Spartan race in a couple of months. The men explained to Ellie about what it entailed. A five-mile run, thirty or so obstacles that consisted of a lot of military-based ideas. Mud pits, tunnel crawls, scaling cargo nets, and swimming across a lake and then sprinting a mile to the finish line. That conversation was the perfect opportunity for Hunter to ask Ellie about the self-defense training.

"Are you going to try and come to our open session self-defense training clinics this upcoming week?" he asked her. She had changed back into her dress, and now a light sweater as the temperature dropped. She looked just as beautiful, but he did like the emerald green bikini better.

"I don't know."

"You should. It's always good to know a few self-defense moves. Even if you learn two or three, it's good," Justice added.

"I can show you some right now. Maybe back in the cabana, just you and I?" Mace teased her, and she blushed.

"I don't think so. Nice try."

Hunter chuckled at Mace. He never saw his brother so forward with a woman and flirty. A jokester, yes, but straight out forward, no.

"I can pick you up after work, and drive you over. Then maybe we could all grab dinner?" Justice suggested.

She took a deep breath and released it as she rubbed her hands together. She was nervous but she didn't turn them down.

"Can I let you know tomorrow? I have a lot going on with this client and it's a demanding project. In fact, I've been pretty tired at the end of the day," she told them.

"Well, this could help you get that energy you're missing. It will be fun, I promise," Hunter told her.

"Okay. Is Tuesday available?" she asked.

"Tuesday is perfect," Hunter said, and then they relaxed until it was time to say good night. That was the hard part. Especially because he knew all he would think about was Ellie, and how one day she would definitely share him and his brothers' bed.

Chapter 7

"A hell of a way to start our Monday, isn't it?" Vin said to Justice as they finished up at their latest crime scene.

Justice shook his head. "This is definitely connected to our case. I don't like how once again Phillips and Renaldo were the last men seen with her."

"Is it coincidence? I don't think so," Vin stated.

"What the fuck? I mean this is insane. Another beautiful brunette tortured and killed. "

"What's with leaving this body in the art district? That's what I'd like to know," Justice stated and Vince looked around them.

"It's an upscale area. Big dealers around here. Could it be some kind of inside message? Maybe a business conflict?" Vin asked.

"It doesn't sit right with me. Maybe we'll get a better idea after we canvas the neighborhood and interview some of the storeowners. It's our only source of info right now."

"Detectives, this is Kelly York. She works as a manager for the art gallery, Venero's. She knows the victim," the other detective told them. Vin and Justice walked over to meet her.

"Hello, Miss York. I'm Detective Lawson and this is Detective Elloy. We understand that you were friends with the victim."

"Yes, her name is Tiffany. My God, I just saw her yesterday afternoon." The redhead covered her mouth and tried to stop the tears from flowing. Vin and Justice took out their notepads.

"How was she when you saw her yesterday?"

"She was happy. She said she landed a great gig for last night. She was psyched because she was a bit behind in her rent."

"Did she say what type of gig this was?"

"No, just that she needed to dress really stylishly and that she was meeting someone, a partner, at the Partridge Hotel. There was some sort of private party in the banquet room."

"How well did you know Tiffany?"

"I've known her for a year or so. She works part time for the manager of the gallery hosting events, private parties when the new artwork comes in."

"Private parties, huh?" Vin asked and looked at Justice.

"Do you know if your friend was working as a prostitute or call girl?"

The redhead crossed her arms in front of her chest and got an attitude. "She wasn't into that anymore. She tried it a few times when things were tough, but no way. Unless there was some serious dough involved, Tiffany would not sell her body."

They gave Kelly their business cards and told her to call them if she heard anything else or remembered anything that could help catch her friend's killer. As they headed toward the door, she yelled to them and headed back. She handed Justice a card.

"I don't know if this has anything to do with her murder. But there's this big shot who comes in, often looking for specific types of art. The owner of the gallery sets up private gatherings for this guy. Tiffany was at one of them a few nights ago. Maybe that's where she met someone, the person who killed her."

"Thank you, Kelly. We'll look into it," Vin said as Justice got into the car. He was staring at the card.

"Who is it? Do you know them?"

Justice looked at Vin. "Looks like this time we're going to have a few questions for Renaldo Sentinel."

"Oh shit."

"Exactly."

* * * *

Ellie was so tired and it was only lunchtime. Renaldo ordered lunch, and of course it came with a bottle of wine. They were discussing the latest updates from the project and had planned on meeting at the end of the week on-site to go over specific details.

"You haven't touched your wine. Is it bad?" he asked her.

"I'm sorry, Renaldo. I'm so tired and if I have that glass of wine, I'm afraid that I'll pass out."

He smiled softly. "You work very hard. If you like, you can lie down for a while on my bed. I'll be sure that no one disturbs you."

She chuckled. "Has that worked for you before?" she asked, standing up and stretching. She was regretting wearing the very high-heeled shoes, but she thought she was going to have to stop at another gallery today and she wanted to look good.

"You'd be surprised, Ellie," he whispered, eyeing her attire over.

"I need to use the bathroom, and then I'm going to get going. Why don't you call that gallery one more time and see if I can stop by on the way back to the office?" she asked him.

"You can't stay and work from here? I can order dinner in."

"Oh, gosh no. Thank you so much for lunch. I'll be right back."

After Ellie finished in the bathroom, she pulled out her cell phone and saw that she'd missed a call from Unc, as well as from Moira. Moira wanted to go to the self-defense classes tonight because she had plans for tomorrow night. There was no way Ellie could make it tonight.

After she washed her hands and absorbed the beauty and elegance of the bathroom, she thought about Renaldo. He was quite the character, but he wasn't boyfriend material. She felt as if he would be the type of man to constantly nitpick about his girlfriend's appearance, dress choices, and would be overbearing. Then she thought about Justice, Hunter, Mace, and Seno. Although they were definitely used to being in charge, being dominant, macho, tough, and gorgeous, they seemed compassionate and caring. She was looking forward to seeing them again.

As she headed down the hallway, absorbing smaller pieces of art in Renaldo's penthouse, she heard male voices and she thought one of them sounded like Justice.

As she rounded the corner she heard Renaldo asking them if they could set up a time to talk and that he had company he was entertaining for the evening.

"Renaldo?" She said his name and then saw both Justice's and Vin's expressions of shock at seeing her there.

"Ellie, honey, these two detectives were just getting ready to leave." He walked closer and placed his arm around her shoulder. She immediately nudged it off and reached for her iPad. She wasn't certain if she should act as if she knew Justice and Vin, however she remembered that he had seen them talking with her outside in the waiting area of Tratorra's.

"Miss Morrison, so nice to see you again. We're sorry to have interrupted your lunch date, but we have some important questions to ask Mr. Sentinel," Vin stated, emphasizing lunch date. Justice looked very angry as he eyed her over.

"Well, you can ask away, I was just getting ready to head back to the office." She started gathering her papers and the iPad. Renaldo stepped toward her and placed both hands on her shoulders.

"I expect an update in a few hours. I can arrange to have dinner set up by seven if you want to return by then."

"Renaldo, I told you that I'm not available for dinner tonight. In regards to getting an update, you'll get it as soon as I finish the designs. Thank you again for lunch."

She walked toward Justice and Vin.

"So nice to see you again. Both of you. Good luck." She headed out of the penthouse.

By the time she pulled her car out of the private parking lot behind the building, her cell phone was ringing.

She saw that it was Unc. "Hi, Unc. Sorry I couldn't return your call, I've been in meetings all morning."

"Not a problem. I was just a bit concerned that's all. Are we still on for lunch Wednesday?"

"Oh God, I'm not sure I can make it. I'm on deadline with this job, I'm meeting some friends tomorrow for a workout."

"A workout? With Moira, Donella, and Jessie?"

"Well, Moira and some guy friends of ours."

"You're dating someone? When did this happen? Does he know about Paul? Why haven't you mentioned this guy until now?"

She chuckled. "I'm not dating anyone. I'm just making some new friends. I'll try my best to make it Wednesday." She could hear the caller ID beeping in indicating she was receiving another call.

"I'm sorry, Unc, I need to take another call. I'll call you tomorrow."

"Be safe. Hope to see you Wednesday."

She disconnected the call and answered the next one just as she approached the exit to the long road that led to her office building.

"Hey, Ellie. You sound happy to hear from me." She nearly missed the parking spot as Paul's voice echoed from her cell phone. She placed the car in park and placed the phone to her ear.

"Ahh, speechless? That's interesting. I didn't mean to shock you."

She took a deep breath and cleared her mind. She needed to act confident and unaffected by him.

"What do you want, Paul?" she asked, pulling the keys into her hand while she got out of the car. She closed her door and then opened the side door to retrieve her briefcase and bag.

"I thought you would be happy to hear from me. It's been so long. Haven't you missed me?"

"Of course not."

"But I heard you're single still. Haven't let another man touch you since me."

She swallowed hard. Her emotions, anger, hatred and fear of this man were beginning to make her shake.

"I have nothing to say to you. Please just leave me alone."

"I can't do that."

"Why the hell not?" she asked, raising her voice as she walked toward the front entrance of the office building. She was going to regret parking so far away from the front entrance tonight when she got out late. But she couldn't get any closer right now. The lot was packed.

"There was a time when you showed respect, and wouldn't dare raise your voice to me. Someone in need of some discipline?" he threatened.

"I don't need shit from you. Leave me alone, or I'm calling the cops." She disconnected the call as she entered the lobby, dropping one bag she was carrying.

"Is everything okay, Ellie?" Lionel asked. He was the security guard on duty at night.

She looked up toward him as he helped her grab the bag that fell.

"Yes. Thank you for helping me. I lost my grip."

"Sounds like a bad phone call. Is everything okay? Is that asshole ex of yours bothering you again?" Lionel asked. She gave him a soft smile. Lionel knew what had happened a year ago because his sister was a nurse at the hospital Ellie wound up in. His sister had provided care for Ellie, and Lionel visited her a few times.

"He just called me now. It is the first time, but I was trying to act tough."

"Well telling him that you were going to call the police is a good thing. You should call that detective."

"I will. Thank you for helping."

"No problem. I'll walk you out tonight if you're staying late. No need to take any unnecessary chances."

"I'm sure I'll be fine."

"I insist. See you later."

She headed toward the elevators with a heavy heart filled with concern. She should call Unc back and ask him what she should do.

Once she was in the privacy of her office, she collapsed down into her chair and held her head.

What am I going to do? I can't keep living in fear like this. I can't let Paul do this to me. Maybe getting that order of protection now is justified and a judge will issue it? I should have recorded the call. Shit.

It was times like these that she wished her uncle Brian was alive still. She wondered why he had to get caught in the middle of that robbery. Why him? Why did that gang of teens decide to do such a thing?

She picked up her phone and called Unc. As Uncle Brian's best friend, Unc had taken over in protecting her, giving her advice, and she knew she could count on him. Unc more than likely felt guilty for not being there that night uncle Brian died. They were supposed to go out to an event together, but Uncle Brian was running late and said he would meet him there. He'd never made it.

Ellie dialed his number.

"Hey Ellie, what's going on?"

"Well, I'm kind of freaking out."

"What is it? Did something happen?"

She told him about the phone call.

"That son of a bitch. We'll track him down. We'll get him locked up."

"Unc, you know as well as I do that isn't going to happen. I have a lot going on right now in my life and with work. I won't let his stupid texts and phone calls bother me. I just wanted someone to know. I'm going to send a text to Detective Ramirez as well."

"Good idea. I'm glad that you called me and told me about Paul calling. The worst thing you could do is keep this all inside. I'm here for you. You know that, right?"

"Of course I do. I have some more things to talk to you about at lunch on Wednesday."

"Oh no, sounds serious. Is there a man involved?"

"Maybe." She felt that anxiety and fear lift slightly.

"Well then, maybe you should bring him along, that way I can meet him?"

She chuckled. "Nice try. I didn't say I'm dating anyone. Not yet, anyway. It's complicated. But I can't talk now. I'll touch base with you tomorrow."

"Okay, you be sure to call me if that shithead contacts you. Also, call Ramirez and let him know about the phone call."

"I will. Good-bye."

"Good-bye."

Ellie felt better as she disconnected the call, but as the evening went on and the office was mega quiet, she started to feel unsafe. Her mind traveled back to when she first met Paul, and how perfect, and caring he seemed. How had things gone so badly? When had she missed the signs of his possessive behavior, his distrust, and his ability to be violent?

She closed her eyes, letting the paperwork go untouched as she remembered that night.

It was raining. She was running late from work and had gotten into an argument with Paul because he wanted her to meet him at a party. From the sound of his voice, he had drunk a lot. She wasn't in the mood, so she told him she was heading home, to bed.

She took a shower and got dressed in a tank and shorts. Her roommates were out partying, so she had the house all to herself.

She watched TV for a little while and then turned off the lights and got into bed.

She had just begun to doze off when she heard the strange noise. It sounded like glass breaking. Before she could get out of the bed to check, he appeared. A man dressed in black.

She tried to run toward the door, but then she heard her name. Turning back toward him, she saw that it was Paul. He was drenched from the rain and staring at her with wild eyes and raw hunger.

"What the hell are you doing? Did you break into my house?"

He grabbed her and she swatted at his hands. "Get off of me. Have you lost your mind?"

The backhand across the mouth shocked her, and then he pulled her by her tank top and threw her onto the bed.

"You think I'm not good enough for you? You like those high-class business men with all the money and the charm more than me?"

"What are you talking about? Don't do this." She cried out. He slapped her again and pulled her down the bed by her legs, getting in between them.

"I can turn you on, baby. I can make you cream yourself right now."

She could see that he was drunk, but there was also this crazy look in his eyes. She didn't understand it. It was like he was getting off on doing this to her.

As he raised his hand, a switchblade popped open.

"You're mine."

She screamed and tried to get away from him but she couldn't. He ripped her tank top open revealing her bare breasts. She struggled to get away, begging him to stop but he wouldn't. He struck her once, twice, three times. She was losing focus. He was so much bigger than her, a large man, nearly six feet tall, big muscles, a corrections officer, he knew how to fight, to stay in control.

When he used the knife to tear off her bottoms, she knew his intentions. She begged him to stop as he ran the tip of the blade across her breast, down her ribs to her mound.

"I wouldn't move, Ellie. This is all mine. No man will ever fuck this pussy, or feel up these tits again. I'm going to make sure you never forget who owns you."

The sound of the office phone ringing brought her out of her daze. She realized that she had been crying, as she wiped away the tears with the back of her hand. She was so lost in remembering, and feeling the pain she had lost track of time and where she even was.

She picked up the phone. "Yes?" she answered.

"Ellie, it's Lionel. There's some guy here to see you with dinner. Seno Lawson. He showed me ID, says he's a criminal analyst, and that you're friends. Is he legit?"

"Oh God, yes. You can send him up. He's a friend, Lionel. Thank you."

"Of course. You call me if you need me."

"I will."

She stood up placing her feet back into the high-heel shoes she wore all day. Her feet protested as she walked over toward the mirror and checked her makeup. It was obvious she was crying, but she hoped that Seno wouldn't be able to tell.

Looking out her office window, she saw him coming through the dark office, looking around with a concerned expression and carrying a box with brown bags in it. She could also see bottles of water.

"Hi, what's all this?" she asked, opening up her office door.

"Nice office. I thought I would surprise you with dinner." He placed the box down onto the desk.

She watched him, absorbing the scent of his cologne, the way his dark Dockers hugged his ass and his thighs, and the way his tight black collared, cotton shirt stretched across bulging muscles. In an instant appreciation, desire, and attraction sparked something within her. Then came the eerie thoughts of only moments ago.

"Hey, what's wrong?"

He was right in front of her, placing one hand on her hip and the other against her cheek. She felt the emotion flood even her eyes.

She smiled softly.

"Thanks for surprising me." She hugged him tight as she willed the tears to remain away. She wouldn't break down in front of him and scare Seno off. She felt so very safe in his arms, and that was what she need right now. Safety.

* * * *

Seno knew something was up. His mind was reeling with numerous questions and concerns. He knew that she had a meeting with some dick who was part of Justice and Vin's investigation. Justice was pissed off after seeing her with the guy, in his penthouse having a lunch meeting with wine and a romantic atmosphere. He also said that this guy touched her, placed his arm around her in a possessive way, but that Ellie nudged him off. His brother was concerned. He had trust issues just like the rest of them.

Seno caressed her back as he held Ellie in his arms. When she pulled back, she tried to sidestep out of his hold, but he wouldn't let her. Looking down into her green eyes, he held her gaze and saw they were red and watery. She had been crying. Who made her cry?

"Okay, let's sit down, have a nice dinner, and talk about what has you so upset."

He let his hand slide down her arm to her hand, squeezing it, he led her toward the desk.

He looked around the room and saw a small table with two chairs.

"We can eat over there. I hope you like what I brought. I know you enjoy your salads, so I ordered grilled chicken over a bed of mixed lettuce with walnut-and-raspberry vinaigrette on the side."

"This is so nice. Thank you," she whispered, taking a seat on the chair as he unwrapped the salads and breadsticks.

She picked up the fork and stared at the salad.

"Something wrong?" he asked her.

"I'm sorry, Seno. I guess I'm not hungry." She stood up and walked over to the desk. He followed her.

"Still full from lunch?" he asked, and her eyes widened. She started to say something and then stopped herself. He raised his eyebrow at her.

"It wasn't what it looked like. It was a business meeting that flowed over into lunch."

"With wine and a romantic atmosphere?" He moved closer, placing his hands on his hips as he absorbed her expression, her body language, and mostly her eyes. He was a criminal analyst, with a knack for seeing things other people didn't see. Ellie was on edge, nervous, upset, and she also felt guilty. Why?

"It wasn't like that."

"You mentioned that already. What was it then? Why do you sound guilty?"

"Guilty? I'm not guilty of anything. Is that what Justice thinks? Does he think I'm intimately involved with Renaldo?"

"He's concerned to say the least. This guy Renaldo and his partner Luke are somehow connected to two murders. So yes, I'd say that Justice is trying to figure out if there is anything romantic going on with you and these men."

"No. No there is absolutely nothing romantic going on between us. They're clients and nothing more."

"Do they know that?"

"I've thought I made my point."

"Then what has you so upset? I can see the fear and the sadness in your eyes, Ellie. Talk to me."

She shook her head. Her cell phone rang.

She was quick to use it as an opportunity to stop their conversation but as she looked at the caller ID, he saw her hesitate and then answer the call.

"Hi, Detective Ramirez. I'm sorry but now isn't exactly a good time. Yes, everything is okay, I'm safe. At the office. No, I'm not alone, a friend is with me. No, we won't need escorts but I appreciate it. Yes, first thing tomorrow morning at the police department. Okay, I appreciate you doing this. I hope not either."

Her one-sided conversation was killing him. This had something to do with her ex. At least it seemed that way from what Hunter told them all about what happened in the cabana the other day.

She said good-bye and disconnected the call. She gripped the desk and hung her head. Seno moved slowly in behind her, wrapped an arm around her waist, and pulled her back against his chest.

"Tell me what's going on. What's this all about?"

"I don't want to, Seno. I don't want you involved or thinking badly of me."

He turned her around, kept his hold around her waist, and pressed her rear against the desk so she couldn't escape his embrace.

"Why would I think badly of you?"

She shook her head. "It's too much. It's too aggravating and I don't want you involved."

"Well, that's not really an option here. If it involves you and whether or not you're in trouble or not safe, then I'm involved. Tell me what that detective wanted."

"I have to go down to the police department tomorrow. To fill out some papers."

He held her gaze.

"What kind of papers?"

"And order of protection. I need to start the process."

He felt his concern immediately flare. He scrunched his eyes, and she lowered her eyes and tried to pull away but he held her tight.

"Who is bothering you? What have they done to scare you? Talk to me, Ellie."

"I said I don't want you involved."

"I am involved. Tell me, now."

"I can handle it."

"Not alone. Together. Now tell me. Is it your ex-boyfriend?"

She nodded her head.

He licked his lower lip and tried to remain calm. "What has he done?"

She explained to him about the text messages and the call.

"What specifically did he say?" She hesitated again and then told him.

He was pissed off. Plain and simple, and when his brothers found out, they would be as well.

"Please don't tell Justice, Hunter, and Mace. They'll get mad at me. Mace and Hunter will insist that I take all those self-defense courses, which I am starting tomorrow. I just don't want to talk about it all."

He reached over and cupped her cheek with the palm of his hand. "Baby, they care about you just as I do. There are no secrets between us. None of us. If we want this relationship to work, then we need to trust one another."

"I told you that I couldn't jump into a relationship like this one. Well, with any kind of relationship."

"Because of this asshole?"

She chuckled. "Yes, because of this asshole. A lot of stuff happened. He hurt me very badly."

"Physically?"

Her eyes filled up with tears and he felt his heart ache for her. Ellie was a gorgeous young woman who should be treated like a goddess. He wanted to know more, everything.

"And mentally, emotionally. God, Seno, you have no idea how hard this has been for me the past year and a half. First, I lost my uncle Brian to a robbery gone badly, and then Paul. Paul came along during my weakest time and went psycho. I was in counseling up until a month ago. It's been so difficult to trust anyone."

He swallowed hard and then hugged her against his chest. He caressed her hair and her back.

"Baby, we said we would go slow, that we can be friends first, but you're going to have to meet us halfway. You can trust us. My brothers and I won't hurt you."

She pulled back, with tears in her eyes and an expression of defeat on her face.

"I don't know if I can, Seno. I don't know how to let the walls down. It's safer to stay locked in."

He held her gaze, looked at her lips.

"I want you, and so do my brothers because we know that you're right for us. Don't you feel it? Isn't the connection, the attraction stronger than this fear of remaining locked inside of yourself?"

A tear rolled down her cheek. "I don't know."

He softly kissed her lips and then pulled back. Her eyes remained closed and he watched her. She blinked them open. "Do you feel it? Can't you see and recognize that I'm one of the good guys?"

She stared into his eyes. He felt the palms of her hands slowly move up his chest. It was like being on pins and needles as he held back from kissing her again. She needed to make the next move. She needed to fight against that wall and let him in.

When she stood up on tiptoes and closed the gap between them to kiss him, he squeezed her tightly and allowed her to pour her emotions into the kiss.

* * * *

Ellie let go for the first time in quite a while. The feel of Seno's embrace, his meaningful words, and the way he pushed for her to fight against being a victim and instead to be the survivor she was, had her taking a huge chance. She kissed him with vigor and excitement, wanting to absorb the sensations of being pressed up against his sexy body while his hands explored her body. She felt his palm move over her ass and squeeze it, so she thrust her hips against him and felt his hard cock against her belly. Seno towered over her, and even that turned her on. When his other hand moved to the hem of her dress and then up her thigh, lifting it against his hip, she moaned into his mouth.

They were on fire, kissing, petting, and exploring.

She felt his fingers move up along the crack of her ass, and she gasped, pulling from his mouth.

"Easy, Ellie," he whispered, using his hold of her thigh and her ass to pull her tighter against him. She was aroused, hungry for more of his touch, yet the fear reminded that the last time a man touched her he forced himself on her and bruised her everywhere. She wanted Seno and his brothers to touch her.

"I can't, Seno. Oh God," she said pulling away, and covering her mouth with her hand to stop herself from losing it.

Strong arms wrapped around her and turned her back to face Seno.

"My God, Ellie. What the hell did he do to you?" She shook her head and he hugged her to him.

"I'm so sorry, Seno. I don't know if this will ever work."

Chapter 8

"The guy has a fucking alibi. I was so hoping that he was our killer," Justice stated.

Vin laughed at Justice as they went over the files from the coroner's report and the evidence from the multiple homicides.

"That would make this case nice and neat, but it isn't. Not with these art galleries playing a role somehow. There has to be more to this," Vin added.

"I'm wracking my brain but nothing is giving," Justice said as he rubbed his eyes after closing the file.

"Let's take a break. So how are things going with Ellie? Did you get to talk to her about yesterday?"

"Nope."

"You're not pissed at her, are you?"

"I was, but then Seno went to go see her last night at work. We didn't want her walking out on her own so late at night."

"And?" Vin asked, leaning back in his chair.

"Seno was upset when he got home last night. It seems that Ellie's ex started texting and calling her. She was supposed to stop in here this morning to fill out some paperwork for an order of protection."

Vin sat forward in his seat. "No way. Shit, that's scary."

"You're telling me. Whatever happened between her and this ex must have really been terrible. It's why she's resistant to us."

"It's why she's been resistant to dating anyone, Justice," Vin said and then looked away from him.

Justice knew that look. Vin knew something.

"Okay, what do you know?"

"Me?" Vin pointed to his own chest.

"Yes, you. I know that look. Did Moira confide in you?"

"Hey, I can't divulge any information Moira may or may not have shared with me in confidence about the woman you and your brothers have your hearts set on bedding."

"Hey, first of all, this is more than just about 'bedding,' Ellie. You know that, so don't even go there."

"How do I know that?"

"Because you and your brothers have been our best friends for years. When have you ever seen the four of us so in tune and interested in the same woman?"

Vin stared at Justice. "Okay, never."

"I rest my case."

"I'm still not going to break a promise."

"Why, because you're afraid Moira will stop sleeping with you and your brothers?"

"First of all, we haven't taken our relationship to that level yet."

Justice raised his eyebrows at Vin. "The three of you have not taken her to bed yet?"

"No, and to be honest, without breaking any sort of confidentiality clause between myself and Moira, she is hesitant to take our relationship to that level yet because of what happened to Ellie."

Justice ground hid teeth and sat forward in his seat. He looked around them to be sure no one could hear.

"It's that bad?"

"Listen, I didn't get the details, just bits and pieces from Moira that indicate the situation was intense and very scary for all of them. I do know that Ellie wound up in the hospital for weeks. She was in counseling up to a month ago. Moira, Donella, and Jessie needed to talk to someone, too. Those four women are close."

Justice rubbed his chin and whispered to Vin. "What do my brothers and I do to help her to see that we would never hurt her, and that she can trust us?"

Vin took a deep breath and then released it.

"I guess all you can do is be patient. If you really care about her, that trust will come. The desire and attraction will be so strong, none of the other stuff will be as powerful."

"God, I want to know what happened to her." He glanced at the computer screen.

Vin sat forward. "Don't do it. Don't look up the case, or Ellie will find out, and that trust you're trying so hard to build will explode in your face."

"Fuck." Justice ran his fingers through his hair and stared at Vin. "When the hell did you become the guru of relationships?"

Vin chuckled and then raised his knuckles and blew over his fingernails in a pompous manner. "Some of us just have it, and others don't."

Justice shook his head.

* * * *

He waited, watching the illegal deliveries go in and out of the warehouse. It was hard to concentrate on the players when all he kept thinking about was her. She came as such a surprise to him, yet she had seemed to be right in front of him for far too long. The moments they shared he cherished. Ties when he couldn't resist so he touched her with thoughts of that moment when they would be one.

The sight of her long brown hair, the sweet smile, and the way her body attracted so many. It pissed him off, made him want to extend his list and end this madness.

He pulled the daisy from the fresh bouquet of flowers. He pressed it under his nose and inhaled then smiled as he thought of her. His desire to have her, make love to her, was overpowering. He needed another. Someone who could satisfy the urge building so deeply in his groin and in his heart.

He looked down at the iPad and watched the surveillance video. He needed to do something, and get to her, make her see that he was the right man and no other. Who was that man walking her out of her office last night? His heart hammered inside his chest. Hadn't she learned yet, that he was the only one for her?

He looked back at the daisy and began to pull the white petals from the lovely flower.

"She loves me, she loves me not, she loves me, she loves me not, she loves me…"

* * * *

Ellie tried to make excuses to get out of going to the self-defense class since Moira went the night before, but her roommates wouldn't have it. Even Unc called and told her to go and that he wanted to hear all about what she learned tomorrow at lunch.

As she entered the training room, she saw a lot of women heading toward one room with some guys dressed in matching black T-shirts. To the left she saw Mace and Hunter. They were talking to a few women with three other men.

Hunter saw her first and waved, then Mace. They waved her over as the other three men walked with the three women to the center of the mat.

"So glad you made it," Mace said, giving her a kiss on the cheek. Hunter kissed her next, and her nerves about whether they would be upset with her disappeared. Now she felt like some lustful woman who had the hots for her two instructors. This could be disastrous.

"Are you ready to learn some basics?" Hunter asked her.

"I guess so. Just take it easy on me. The only workouts I'm used to are jogging and some kickboxing classes."

Hunter raised his eyebrows up at her. "We can incorporate that into some moves, no problem. Come on. We're going to use the other room. These mats are being used by the regulars."

As she followed them into the other room, their size and their extra large bodies became her mind's and her eyes' focus. Considering that most of the time they had spent together she was wearing high-heeled shoes, right now both men towered over her and she was worried about how intimidating it felt.

As they started talking with her, setting up some scenarios she thought she could handle, that bit of anxiety and fear started to bubble in her gut.

"Okay, first of all we need to see instinctually what you would do and how you would react in a series of different situations. That being said, don't think of it as friendly and that you know us. Pretend you don't know us. We're strangers, and you need to protect yourself. Got it?" Hunter asked, and she looked at both of them.

"You're both not going to attack, are you?" she asked. Mace stood back with his arms crossed in front of that sexy big chest of his. The muscles in his upper arms were stretching the material making it roll up slightly. They both had rock-hard abs. She could tell because she was so close to them.

"We're going to simulate an attack to see your response. Okay, let's go over the first scenario." Mace had her focus on him as Hunter did something behind her. Mace told her what to do and that she was walking from her office to her car at night, and the parking lot lights were dim.

As she began to walk, she sensed someone behind her, and when she turned to look, there was Hunter wearing a hoodie, he grabbed her from behind and she automatically used her elbow to thrust into his gut and then turned out of his arms.

"Very good. Perfect. You immediately retaliated, you got out of his hold, but the only thing you didn't do was scream for help and then take off. You need to draw attention to yourself. Get out of his hold, scream, and run," Mace stated.

She felt her throat clogging up, and she tried to push bad memories out of her head. This was practice, a way to prepare to defend herself if someone went after her. *Would Paul come after me again? Could I stop him from hurting me, taking what he wanted, raping me?*

They went over a few other scenarios, and each time she used a move she knew or one they taught her. Every time Hunter or Mace showed her the steps to the moves where they had to press their bodies against her and show her step-by-step, it was difficult to follow. Somehow she did and she started to feel comfortable with them.

"Okay, now we're going to try something different. A little bit scarier," Mace stated.

"Like what?" she asked, looking to each of them, and then Hunter walked over toward a basket and pulled something out.

"What do you do if the person attacking has a weapon?"

"Cooperate?"

"If they mean to kill you and you have a chance at escaping, what do you do?"

"Whatever I need to in order to escape?"

"Exactly."

Ellie took a deep breath and prepared for another mock attack from Hunter. However, this time when he approached from behind and she countermoved, she saw the knife, and freaked out. "Okay, we're done." She started walking quickly toward the bench where she threw down her sweatshirt and bag.

"Whoa, what are you doing? We're not finished," Mace stated. She didn't want to fight with them but also didn't want to face the feelings this situation brought on.

"Ellie, it's okay to be afraid. Lots of women become anxious, uncomfortable even, with this type of scenario. But if you can just push through that, it could save your life," Mace told her as Hunter stood next to him, still holding the knife.

"Could you put that away please?"

"It's not real."

"It looks real."

"It isn't. Look at it." Hunter lowered his hand palm forward with the knife sitting there for her to take.

She shook her head.

"I know that knives scared you. You mentioned that at the party. I just remembered."

"Why does it scare you so much?" Hunter asked.

"Don't, Hunter."

"Don't what?" he asked, stepping closer. She looked down and felt so compelled to explain, yet fearful of his reaction. Of their reactions. She stared at the loose-fitting pants Hunter wore, and she could see that he was wearing a prosthetic device. One leg looked thicker than the other. But with his big muscles and tattoos bursting from his shirt, she could only focus on how attracted she was to him. She glanced at Mace, stern, crew cut hair, blue eyes and muscles galore, the man looked like a weapon. This gave her more anxiety she didn't know how to redistribute to a positive aspect.

Hunter pressed his fingers under her chin encouraging her to look up at him.

She locked gazes with his green eyes.

"Seno told us about the order of protection, and how your ex is bothering you again."

Her eyes widened.

"It's okay. We're pissed off, and we're worried. Maybe we pushed a little too much for you to learn some moves today that you're not ready for," Mace added. She couldn't believe this. They thought they were at fault for her anxiety and freaking out. They were trying to help her.

"No, it wasn't that. I was fine until the knife, Hunter." She sat down on the bench. Mace knelt down in front of her and placed his hand on her knee. The tingling feeling from where his palm touched all the way to her pussy had her adjusting her position on the bench. Hunter took a seat next to her and kept his one leg stretched out straight.

"Why such a fear? Did your ex carry a knife, or threaten you with one?" Mace asked, and she felt as if a ball were lodged in her throat. She couldn't go on like this. She liked them both. She liked Justice and Seno as well. Each of them had characteristics she wanted in a man, a mate. She didn't want to blow the chance at something special.

"I haven't spoken to anyone about it except for the counselor the doctor suggested." She clasped her hands together and stared at her lap and then looked at Mace.

"I know you collect knives. I wouldn't ask you to stop doing that because of me, but knives scare me. I was attacked months ago and my attacker used a knife to get me to cooperate."

"Oh Jesus, baby. I'm so sorry," Mace said, squeezing her knee and then moving up to sit beside her.

Hunter placed his arm behind her shoulders and she leaned back. She looked at him.

"Where were you attacked?" he asked.

She pulled her bottom lip between her teeth. She could do this. She could give them some details, just not all of them.

"Late at night, in my bedroom."

His green eyes suddenly looked darker, his hand clutched her shoulder.

"Baby, you were—"

She nodded her head and he stopped talking and ran his hand over his face. Mace placed his hand against her cheek and she looked at him. He seemed genuinely upset.

"No wonder you've been scared to let us touch you."

"I want you to," she blurted out, and Mace squinted his eyes at her. She looked at Hunter and he held the same serious expression. She looked back at Mace.

"I haven't been with anyone since it happened. I honestly never met anyone I wanted to be intimate with, until I met you and your brothers. That scares me for a whole lot of other reasons that even if I hadn't been attacked and assaulted I would surely still feel."

"It is a bit of a different relationship, Ellie, but it's also very special. Four men to cater to your every whim, and to protect you, care and provide for you," Hunter whispered as he caressed her neck by her ear.

She looked down at her hands.

"I want that. I want to feel safe and protected, loved and cherished. I don't want to be afraid anymore. I think that's what scares me about liking you and your brothers."

"What's that?" Mace asked.

"I'm afraid that I'll want too much. That I'll become dependent on each of you and lose myself, my identity, and perhaps fail at recognizing the signs that say it's over and the trust is lost."

"Baby, there are no guarantees in life. But isn't it better to try, to see where it leads, and perhaps have faith that the bond formed grows over time and nothing can break it?" Mace asked her.

"How do I do that? How do I take a chance when I'm so fearful?" Hunter placed his hand against her cheek. She locked gazes with him.

"I know exactly how you feel. That fear of failing, of never feeling whole again? I get it. I've been there. Hell, I've conditioned myself to not think or remember what it was like to have both legs. I've learned to deal with it, to overcome any obstacles or stereotypes that are out there because of the need I had inside to be whole again. You can't give up, or not even try to open your heart again because of the past."

She felt the tear roll down her cheek. He was so strong, so encouraging. "I wish I could be like you. Have your strength, your motivation and determination to succeed and to enjoy what life sends my way."

"You can do it. We've all faced obstacles in our lives. We've been scarred on the inside or even the outside, but we don't give up," Mace stated.

She thought about what they were saying. They were so kind, so compassionate.

"I guess there's this feeling that you could hurt me, and the fact that there are four of you, and you are each so intimidating and filled with muscles, it adds to the fears I have."

"But we would never use our strength or our abilities to cause you pain or harm," Hunter told her.

"But the fear is there, Hunter. It's right there making me remember the night I was attacked, and the fact that a man I trusted did what he did to me."

"Who attacked you, and forced themselves on you that night?" Hunter asked.

"Paul, my boyfriend."

"Motherfucker," Hunter exclaimed.

"And this fucking guy is bothering you now? He's the one you have the order of protection against?" Mace asked, standing up and running his fingers through his hair.

"Please calm down. Please don't do this. I need you to be calm and to understand."

Hunter took both of her hands into his own. He gave them a squeeze, indicating for her to look him in the eyes.

"We will not let this asshole touch you. We're going to work this out. We're going to prove to you that with us is where you belong. That jerk broke the trust between you and corrupted it in the worse possible way. He is not a man. He's a loser. We want you in our lives, and in our beds. We'll fight for you, because you're everything we've ever wanted and more." He leaned forward and kissed her, taking her breath away and stealing her heart in a flash.

* * * *

Mace pulled Ellie into his arms and kissed her as Hunter opened her car door. The evening's events had taken a crazy turn but seemed to have ended in a positive. She kissed him freely, went limp in his arms, and even moaned as he pressed her ass against him so she could feel how hard she made his cock. He wanted her with him or one of his brothers, not alone, not vulnerable to her asshole ex-boyfriend. There had to be something they could do to help her more.

As he released her lips, she hugged him tight.

Pulling back, she shyly looked at him and Hunter.

"Sorry if I ruined your usual routine of teaching self-defense."

"Baby, tonight was the best session we ever had."

"Why is that?"

"Because not only did we get to roll around with our sexy woman, but we also got to kiss you and move in the right direction toward progressing in this relationship," Mace teased as he slid his palm along her ass and then her hips. She blushed as she swatted his hand away.

"Call us as soon as you get home, okay?" Hunter pointed at her with authority.

She smiled. "Yes, sir, I promise." She then got into her car. After she pulled away, Hunter and Mace headed toward Mace's truck.

"We should follow her."

"And risk freaking her out?" Mace asked as they got into the truck.

"I really don't care. You heard her. Sure, she didn't tell us everything but I got the gist of it. Her boyfriend breaks into her bedroom at night, holds her at knifepoint, beats her up, rapes her, and now that same asshole is stalking her. Fuck yeah, I think we should follow her home."

Mace looked at him, feeling that same anxiety, but trying not to freak out.

"Fine, let's do it. Then we need to talk with Justice and Seno. They need to know the deal before Ellie comes over for dinner Friday night."

"At least she said yes, to coming over," Hunter said as Mace pulled out of the parking lot and sped up until he was a good distance from Ellie's sports car yet out of her view.

Mace couldn't believe how nervous and angry he felt.

"Are you feeling what I'm feeling?" he asked Hunter.

"Like hunting down that fucker and showing him what it feels like to be beaten and held at knifepoint?" Hunter replied.

Mace chuckled. "That answers my question. But you know we need to be rational here. Any show of aggression can push Ellie away."

Hunter was silent and then turned to look at Mace as they both saw Ellie turn into her development. "I know. I'll do anything to make her happy and to gain her trust. She needs us, as much as we all need her, you know that, right?"

"I know it, and so do Justice and Seno. We'll talk tonight. She's the one. She's definitely the one."

Chapter 9

Ellie was working at her desk in the office when her cell phone rang. She had an hour before she needed to leave to meet Unc for lunch at Ray Ray's. Peeking at the caller ID, she saw that it was Moira. She answered the call.

"Hey, I didn't get to talk to you this morning before you left for work. How did the self-defense instructions go?"

"They were informative." She felt her chest tighten. She also felt kind of embarrassed, yet relieved, to have shared some of her experience with Hunter and Seno. She was certain they would tell Justice and Mace.

"Informative? What does that mean? Did they teach you anything or did you wind up underneath one of them on the mat making out like I did when Sam tried to teach me some self-defense moves?"

Ellie chuckled. "Well, I did kiss them both."

"Both Hunter and Seno? Yes!" Moira exclaimed, and Ellie laughed.

"It kind of turned into a mess, but ended well, I guess."

"What do you mean?"

"Well, things were going great, and I was learning some moves, and they seemed impressed with my abilities to evade being attacked from behind."

"But?"

"But then they changed the scenario, and Hunter came at me with a knife."

"Oh shit. Damn, Ellie, are you okay? Did you have nightmares last night?"

Ellie walked toward the window and looked out at the parking lot. It was a rainy day and rather gloomy. Usually these days made her feel down, but today she felt optimistic. It was because of the men.

"Actually, I did have a rough night, but every time I felt trapped, and as if I couldn't escape, I imagined one of the guys. Hunter, Justice, Mace, and Seno would pop into my head. It's wild, Moira, but I really like them. I think they're good men that I can trust."

"That's fantastic. The best news I've heard in a long time. Which brings me to the other issue. What about Paul?"

"I filled out the paperwork for the order of protection. The problem is that his threats were not recorded on my cell phone, just text messages which do not incriminate him at all. He asked what was up, how are you, nice things. The phone conversation is my word against his word."

"But what about what he did to you? He served time for that."

"Moira, he was in jail for a week before his lawyers got him out and the judge ordered for him to receive counseling for anger management and to do community service. His record as a corrections officer and the fact he was a hero during the riot beat out what he did to me."

"So what are you going to do now? Have you told the men about this?"

"I'm just going to live my life and just keep looking over my shoulder. What else can I do? As far as Justice and his brothers are concerned, I'm not going to get them involved. As is, last night Seno and Hunter followed me home because I told them about what Paul did to me."

"You told them everything?"

"Of course not. I told them enough for them to get the gist of it. I don't need to relive the details."

"You can trust them. They like you a lot. They're worth the risk, you know?"

"I like them a lot, too. But liking four men, dating them, sleeping with them, is truly freaking me out."

"Of course it is. A ménage relationship is very different and powerful. It's not something to jump into blindly. You have a lot of legitimate concerns that you need to share with them. I say just see where it leads. If it feels good, and you feel safe, take the chance. You deserve to be loved."

"Thanks, Moira. I'd better go. I need to finish up a few things before I head out to meet Unc for lunch."

"Oh great. Tell him I said hello. Oh crap. You didn't tell him about them yet did you?"

"Of course not. I was planning on telling him today. He's been a rock for me. Uncle Brian would be so happy to know that Unc is watching over me."

"Well, they were best friends and he treats you like his family. Good luck with telling him that you may be engaging in sexual activity with four very large, dominant men who are retired soldiers and involved in law enforcement."

"Thanks a lot. I think I'll leave out the sex part."

Moira chuckled. "Unc is a very attractive older man, I am certain he will question whether his favorite girl is able to handle such a relationship."

"Well, I won't be able to answer that question for him."

"Why not?"

"Because I'm not certain of the answer. Wish me luck and I'll see you later tonight."

"Good luck," Moira said and then chuckled before she disconnected the call.

As she started putting files away, and then sent out a few e-mails, she heard the knock at her door. Looking up, she was surprised to see her boss. "Hi," she stated, and he smiled.

"Are you avoiding getting together for meetings with our client, Mr. Sentinel?"

She was shocked at his question but recovered quickly as she stood up from the seat. “I cannot get work done at his penthouse nor do I think it professional either.”

Ernest Westerly walked further into the office. “Has he tried something?”

“You mean like to kiss me? No. Flirting, pressing against me, placing his hands on my waist or shoulders and squeezing? Yes. But that I can handle. I just think that I can get more done here and at the site. As a matter of fact, I have a lunch appointment in thirty minutes and then I’m headed over to the job site. I am supposed to meet Renaldo and Luke there.”

“Okay, that’s wonderful. The restaurant is coming together quickly. Renaldo is hoping to open in two months.”

“Two months? How the heck can that happen when he keeps changing the designs?”

“Well, that’s where you come in. You need to be there with him to pull on the reigns and get him to stop making these outrageous changes.”

“Me? How the hell am I supposed to do that?”

“By spending more time with him and whispering into his ear how perfect everything is going. Keep him focused on the art he enjoys so much. In fact, he called a little while ago asking if you could meet him at the art gallery downtown. He tried your cell phone but never got voice mail. Maybe call him and meet him there after your lunch date?”

“I was on the phone with Moira. I didn’t hear the beep. I’ll call him on the way out and meet him there. Does the manager have the paintings we were looking for?”

“Supposedly she does. Let me know how things go. Talk to you later.”

As she grabbed her bags and closed up her computer, she thought about Renaldo. He didn’t seem like such a bad guy, but he did seem to have a hard time taking "no" for an answer. But she had a job to do, so why fight it?

* * * *

"I wanted this to go off without a hitch. What the hell is up with these women showing up dead?" Luke asked Renaldo as they sat in Renaldo's penthouse.

"I don't know. They were sent by the company so we had a good idea of our investments."

"Yeah, well someone is either onto our investments and fucking with us, or we suddenly have some serious bad luck. If those detectives search deep enough, they'll find out those women were not your typical high-price call girls."

"No, they won't, Renaldo. As far as the cops are concerned, they can dig all they want. Those women chose their professions. The cops won't find out about the international prostitution exchange. The plan has worked for a decade. It's foolproof."

"Nothing is foolproof, and nothing lasts forever. I think it may be wise to start slowly pulling our investments from this operation."

"Are you kidding me? This is a multibillion-dollar operation. I don't want to give up those kinds of funds."

"Well, you may have to, Luke. Women who we have slept with to sample the product are being killed. It's not me killing them. Is it you?"

"Hell no."

"Well then, we need to start thinking of downsizing our investments. I have a bad feeling about this. I've screwed over a lot of people. Hell, I killed a few to get where I am. I'm not going to lose it all over some worthless whores."

"Or some jerk who could set us up to the fall for the entire operation. That would be life in prison with no parole," Luke added.

"They could just put a bullet in my head. I would never survive that." Just then Renaldo's cell phone rang. He answered it and smiled.

"Sure thing, Ellie. That will be perfect, thanks for calling me back. I'll see you there."

"Well?" Luke asked, and Renaldo smiled.

"That was Ellie. She's going to meet me at the gallery in two hours." Renaldo fixed his tie as he looked into the hallway mirror.

"You really like her, huh?" Luke asked.

"What's not to like? She's gorgeous, sexy, classy, and smart, and most importantly she fits."

"Fits what?"

"In my plans to sweep her away to Venice and have my way with her perfect body."

"Why, when you can have anyone?"

"Because, she could be my greatest investment. By the time I'm done conditioning her, I'll make a lot of money just off her assets in Europe."

"Are you fucking crazy? You'd prostitute her out? I thought you meant to keep her for yourself."

"I could see myself with her for a very long time. But you know me. Things grow old to me quickly. I've never really committed my heart to anyone. And she has a lot to offer the right man. If I can profit off of that, then I'll do it. Now let me get ready. I want to be sure that every moment I spend with her gives me insight as to how to help mold her into the woman I need her to be. Perhaps by next week, she'll be in my bed, and I'll truly have an understanding of her marketability."

* * * *

"Say that again?" Unc asked her. He was shocked. Utterly speechless when she told him about Justice, Mace, Seno, and Hunter.

She first explained about Paul and then the inability to get the order of protection. He was very upset.

"I know it's a lot to take in, Unc. But I really need someone to talk to about this. I'm scared."

He leaned back and stared at her. "Four men? How? How could this even be a possibility after what Paul did to you? I don't think it's a smart idea. I think you're focusing on their professions and what they stand for as American soldiers. What if they're not so perfect and they hurt you? Paul could have killed you that night, and he was one man with a knife."

She ran her finger tip over the rim of her ice tea glass.

"I know. I've been thinking about all those things, yet I still come back to my feelings for them. I like them a lot. I've never considered a ménage before. Hell, I wasn't even sure that I would ever want to date or be interested in dating. But I like them, each of them, for different reasons, but also the same ones."

"Like what? Because they're highly trained, they have big muscles and sexy bodies?" he asked and she felt her cheeks warm.

"Well, that is a definite plus. But I guess it's how safe I feel when I'm with them. I don't feel on edge except well, my anxiety about the attraction."

"Have you slept with them?" he asked, shocking her. "Don't look so stunned. Any person's first reaction to finding out that their friend, a woman, was considering engaging in a ménage relationship would focus on the sex. Have you been able to get that close to them?"

She shook her head.

He leaned back in his chair, stared at her, and released a sigh. "But you want to?"

"I like them. I like how Justice is so strong and authoritative. He acts tough but he really is a softy. I like how Seno is meticulous and calm. He's always so in tune to emotions and has this way of watching over me. Then there's Mace. He's such a character. He makes me laugh, he understands my obsession with collecting shoes because he collects, too."

"Shoes?" he asked, and she chuckled.

"No, he collects John Wayne memorabilia, and swords and knives."

"Swords and knives?" He raised his voice and sat forward.

"I know. It's crazy, and I hate knives, but I trust him, Unc. I trust the others, too. And then there's Hunter. "

"Which one is he, the perfect soldier or the detective?"

"No, Justice is a detective, Hunter teaches self-defense, and works in computers for the government. He's an amputee. He lost part of his leg while serving in the Marine Corps."

"Damn. That's a lot to handle. You're not turned off by that, or fearful that he may be mentally unstable?"

"What do you mean? Because it's difficult to face being an amputee and trying to live a normal life? Hell, you should see him, Unc. He's incredible. He took first place in this special race on Saturday. He was the first amputee to ever accomplish that. Hunter does not know the words 'give up.' He's a fighter, a survivor like me."

She lowered her eyes to her lap and then Unc took her hand.

"You are a survivor and a fighter. I just want what's best for you. Brian would want me to ensure that you were safe, loved, and well cared for."

"You've been a great friend," she replied as her cell phone began ringing. She pulled her hand away from his to answer the call.

"Okay, I can bring the painting to the site. Can you have them wrap it really good? It's raining so hard out there. Great, see you then."

"What's going on?"

"Oh, it's the client I'm working for. He's really into artwork and special one-of-a-kind pieces for his new restaurant chain. You probably know him, Renaldo Sentinel."

"Sentinel, the multimillionaire?" he asked.

"Yes."

"That guy has a reputation with the ladies. He also was questioned by the police in regards to those murdered women. I don't like this, Ellie."

"It's okay. Justice said that Renaldo had alibis. He doesn't believe Renaldo or his assistant, Luke, to be the killers. I'm sure the detectives will figure things out."

"But this guy Renaldo is a slimeball from what I've heard. Has he tried anything with you?"

"Unc, I handled it. He knows I'm not interested."

"But you're meeting him now, at the gallery? For what?"

"It's work related. We need to go over some other pieces that came in from Venice. Then we're headed to the work site. The builders are already Sheetrocking everything and adding all the decorative finishing touches. I have to make sure that Renaldo doesn't go changing things last minute. We're on a deadline and I have the commercials ready to air and the cost below budget. If I can make the company some more money, then my bonus will be higher. It's hell, but it will be worth it."

"You work so hard. You be sure to let me know if this guy tries anything. I mean I know now you have four other men who you'll go to first, but I want to know."

"Unc, it's only the beginning stages with me and the guys. I need you in my life. You're my rock, the one person I could always count on, just like Uncle Brian."

Unc smiled. "I'm always here for you, Ellie. Even if everything and everyone else fails to come through, I'm here."

She smiled as she stood up and grabbed her things.

"Be careful driving. It's really coming down hard."

"I will. I'll talk to you soon."

* * * *

Sam was talking with one of the arresting officers on the side of the main highway. They had a large tractor trailer pulled over, and a team of officers breaking open the locks on the back of the truck. The driver of the vehicle failed to provide proper identification and registration for the vehicle when the highway patrol officers pulled him over for a broken taillight.

As they got the doors open, and shone the lights into the back, they were surprised by the contents. The driver was kicking the windows and doors from inside the patrol car as officers opened up the doors and climbed up into the truck.

Sam shone his light toward the rear of the container. He felt the shock to his heart as three women sat tied up and gagged in the back. Around them were various crates and pieces of fine art.

Thirty minutes later, he was on the phone with Vin and Justice.

"You're going to want to come out here and see this. Looks like Phillips and Sentinel may not be so detached from those murdered women."

"What's going on?" Vin asked, and Sam explained what he found.

"Shit, Sam. Ellie is at the gallery now with them. Justice got off the phone with her an hour ago."

"Well, tell him to call her and to get her out of there pronto. I've got officers heading there now to bring Phillips and Sentinel in for questioning. This doesn't look good for them."

"I'm on it," Vin stated and Sam looked at the women as the paramedics provided first aid for them. They were very pretty, and young. But as they tried to talk to them and ask them questions, they were too scared to respond. Something big was brewing here. Something connected to Justice and Vin's investigation, and now Sam would help them figure out what.

* * * *

Ellie was on her way out of the gallery even though Renaldo tried to talk her into going out for dinner. As he looked at new art that arrived to the gallery hours before, he told her how beautiful she was and how many men would find her to be appealing. It was so odd, and as if he were describing her assets as if she were art to be displayed. It made her feel like the man wasn't even human but so obsessed with money and getting something from everyone he met, that he had no soul. She was relieved when her phone rang as she attempted to leave for the third time and Renaldo pulled her into his arms. He was going to kiss her and she shoved away from him.

"Renaldo, I'm not interested in you in that way. Now, I'm leaving and I need to take this call. You can drop this picture at the site. I'm heading to my office to work." She answered the call as she popped open the umbrella and headed to her car. It was really raining hard.

"Where are you?" Justice asked her firmly. Not a hello, how are you? A roar. Something was wrong.

"I'm just leaving the gallery and heading to the office. What is going on?"

"Good. Is Renaldo following you?"

"No. Why?"

"Just get away from him. There's been a break in the investigation and until I know what I'm dealing with, I need to know you're safe and away from Renaldo and Luke."

"No problem there, I was happy to leave that jerk back there." She pulled the car out of the parking lot and onto the road. It was dark out, too. The bad weather really put a damper on the day.

"Did he try something? Did he touch you?" Justice asked, sounding angry.

"No. I'm fine, Justice. You don't need to worry."

"I do worry. I'm going to call Mace, and ask him to meet you at the office."

"That's not necessary."

"Just drive carefully and he'll meet you there. It's as precaution. I'll talk to you later."

Ellie disconnected the call and focused on driving through the rain. Justice sounded so upset, and it scared her. Could Luke and Renaldo have something to do with those women being murdered?

As she headed down the main roadway and then took the turn to the right a few blocks from her office, she noticed a car following close behind her. At first she thought it might be Mace, but that wasn't his truck. This truck looked white and Mace's was black.

Before she made it into the parking lot, the truck pulled alongside her, nearly causing her to drive off the road and onto the shoulder. Her car was a collector's car, and worth a lot of money. Her uncle took such good care of it and so did she. Who was this jerk?

He let her by and he went in a different direction in the parking lot. She pulled into a spot and waited as the truck stopped. She grabbed her things realizing that the guy was in some kind of hurry to get inside. Cursing about what a moron he was and that he could have caused damage to her vehicle, she grabbed her one bag and got out of the car. She opened the umbrella and locked her car then started to hurry across the parking lot in between cars.

"Ellie!" She heard her name, and instantly turned, but it was the voice that had her shocked and frozen in place.

The rain was poured down around her, wetting her stockings, her heels, and the hem of her dress. He threw back his hood and started yelling at her.

"How could you do this to me? All I wanted to do was talk with you, try to make things right."

"Paul, what are you doing here? Get away from me." She turned and started walking faster toward the building and in between cars, when he pulled her back by her arm. She swung at him dislodging his hold on her sleeve, but also lost the umbrella as the wind picked up and the rain immediately drenched her.

"I want to talk to you. Don't you walk away from me." He grabbed her and pressed her against the car, setting the alarm on it off. He looked so crazy, almost like that night he attacked her.

"Please leave me alone."

He stared at her as he held her arm, but didn't go to hit her. He looked over her body and then slowly reached toward her light sweater, pushing aside the material. She shoved his hand away and he shoved his body against hers, grabbing her face between his hands.

"I've been going through hell because of you. No woman will come near me. None of my friends want to hang out with me. All I have is my fucking job, around criminals, monsters."

"Then you should fit right in. Let me go. You can't do this. You have no right touching me."

He grabbed her hips and shoved his body against hers, rocking his hips hard. She cried out and tried shoving her hands against his chest, but he grabbed them with his one hand and held them above her head. The rain was soaking her, the sting of metal wedged against her back enraged her. He continued to thrust his hips, and then used his other hand to press against her breast right before he crashed his mouth down on hers.

She was scared, so scared as she tried to fight him off. When his lips left hers and moved along her neck, she knew she couldn't fight him with strength, and needed to make him think she was giving in.

"Slow down, Paul. Please."

He paused, his mouth inches from her chin as he stared into her eyes. "This is what you like. You want it hard and rough. You like to pretend you don't, but this turns you on. I'll never let you go. I'll never give you up."

He moved his hand up over her breast under the sweater and she closed her eyes, and tried to remember what Hunter and Mace taught her.

He shoved her hard, groped her and squeezed her, causing bruises, she just knew it.

"Get away from me!" she yelled at him.

He forearmed her to the jaw, her head went back and hit the car window. She heard more sirens, and it drew Paul's attention to the right as he lightened his hold on her.

"You're coming with me," he stated with his teeth and mouth against her neck and hair, sending chills through her body. She was crying, shaking, trying to get up enough courage and anger to defend herself and stop him from taking her. The sirens grew louder, and she knew help was coming. Somehow, it had to be for her. As he released her hands and sucked hard against her neck while fondling her breast, she made her move. She shoved her fingers into his eye sockets and then raised her knee up hard and fast. He roared in anger but released her and she started to run, he grabbed at her dress, ripping the material, causing her to fall to the hard wet ground and right into a puddle of water.

"Help!" she screamed as she struggled to get away from his hold when suddenly he released her.

Turning back, she was shocked to see Hunter on top of Paul punching him and then pulling his arms behind his back. Police cars were pulling onto the scene, men in uniform, and Lionel was there pointing, running to her. She saw the police officers grabbing Paul from Hunter's hold and cuffing him as Mace ran to her and squatted down next to her. He cupped her face between his large hands and she felt him shaking. "Are you okay? Oh God, you're hurt."

She cried out as Mace pulled her into his arms and held her tight. She clung to him, climbed up his body, and squeezed his neck as she continued to cry hysterically against his neck. She needed him. The safety and security of Mace's big, strong arms, the scent of his familiar cologne to block out everything that just happened.

She felt Hunter behind her, covering her with something, a blanket, a poncho, she didn't know and she didn't care. She kept inhaling against Mace, trying to make his scent, his masculinity take away Paul's saliva against her skin, the smell of his sweat, his evilness. Mace squeezed her to him and carried her away and into the office building.

"Baby, we need to look you over, to see if you need medical attention," Hunter whispered as he caressed her back.

"No. No hospital. Please just hold me. I need you. I need both of you. I want to go home." She could hear their cell phones ringing and Hunter cursing behind her. He was scared, angry, and upset. He and Mace saved her. They got to her in time. She realized in that moment when Paul was grabbing at her body, threatening her, and trying to weaken her resolve, that she was a different person than a year ago. She was a different woman than weeks ago. She was a fighter. She was also in love with Mace, Hunter, Seno, and Justice. She could have lost the opportunity to love them and to see where their connection led. All because of Paul, and the control he still had on her until tonight.

She closed her eyes and took a deep, unsteady breath. As she looked around her, she saw Hunter and Mace, then the police, Lionel and other staff members including her boss, waiting to see if she was okay.

"I want to go home. Please, Mace, Hunter, take me home."

* * * *

Mace carried Ellie up to the bedroom. After filling out the police report and pressing charges, they were relieved that she was safe and that she accepted their desire for her to come back to their place tonight. She was resistant until she spoke with her roommates and they insisted she needed to feel safe and protected. She clung to him now, still shaking, but no longer crying. She refused to go to the hospital to get checked out. She had a nasty bruise along her jaw, and red marks against her neck and chest that led under her ripped blouse. He didn't even want to think about how far Paul had gotten in assaulting her.

He thought about what he and Hunter saw as they pulled up into the parking lot at her office building. A man dressed in black had her pressed against the side of a car, her arms pinned above her head and then his mouth against hers. When they jumped out of the car and saw her fighting him off and then trying to run, screaming for help as he grabbed her making her fall to the ground, he had never been so angry and scared.

Slowly he lowered her to her feet, and she shivered.

He cupped her cheek as Hunter and Seno watched her reaction.

"We need to get these wet things off of you. Seno can get the shower started, nice and warm to heat you up. Okay?" He reached for her sweater. She shook her head and clutched it tightly.

His heart ached. "Baby, you need to. Do you want to go into the bathroom and do it yourself?" Hunter asked her. She looked at him and shook her head.

"What do you need us to do?" Seno asked her. "We'll do anything."

"I can't stop shaking. I need you to hold me." A tear rolled down her cheek.

"We'll help you," Mace said just as they heard the heavy footsteps. Justice ran into the bedroom.

"Ellie?" He said her name and went to her then paused a few inches in front of her.

"I'm okay, Justice." She stepped closer and he hugged her tightly.

A few seconds passed and he pulled back holding her by her arms. "You're soaked. You need to get out of these clothes or you'll catch a cold."

"I know." She didn't move and they all just waited to see what she wanted them to do. She reached for Justice's hand and pulled it to her cheek. She closed her eyes and hugged it to her.

"Help me, Justice. Help me feel safe, please," she said.

* * * *

Ellie needed them. She wanted their touch, their mouths on her, their caresses and bodies. She wanted to soak up their cologne, their manliness and wear them like body armor. It was so wild and crazy, but she did. She felt almost desperate now. It was like she could have lost the opportunity to get to love them if Paul had been successful.

Mace, Seno, and Hunter stood around her, and Justice began to undo the small buttons on her sweater. The others helped pull off the wet material and drop it to the rug. Behind her Hunter unzipped the dress and lay soft kisses on her bare, damp shoulder as he peeled the material away. She closed her eyes and kept her arms at her sides as they removed the dress.

"Damn it," Justice whispered and she popped her eyes open and saw him staring at her chest. She looked down, chin to chest and saw what appeared to be finger marks, just as Hunter unclipped the bra. The garment fell to the floor as did the remainder of the dress. Now she stood in thong panties, and her very high heels.

Justice leaned forward, gently cupped her breast, and kissed where the marks lay.

"You're so lovely, Ellie," Mace whispered and then Hunter wrapped an arm around her waist from behind and kissed her neck. She gasped and a small cry released from her lips.

"Are you sure you can handle this right now?" Hunter asked her. "We understand if the intimacy scares you."

She shook her head. "Please. Take his scent away, his touch. I could have lost having this with you. Please, Hunter," she whispered.

Seno lowered down and licked across her other nipple, making her shiver.

"She needs to get warmed up in the shower," Mace stated. She looked at him and held his gaze.

"Later, I want this. I need this, Mace," she told him, baring her desire with no more reservations or fears. Paul's attack and Renaldo's attempt at seducing her into bed made her see what was right in front of her. Four perfect men she trusted and desired and who proved they could keep her safe.

"Are you sure, Ellie? We don't want you to have any regrets," Seno said as he rose up and cupped her cheek.

"No regrets. Please, make love to me."

Hunter released his hold of her and for a moment she thought he didn't want her. But then he pulled off his shirt and then his pants before sitting down on the bed. She caught sight of his muscles, the tattoos, and of course his leg. He caught her expression and looked hurt but then calm.

He started to remove the device and she watched him, knowing that she cared for him so much and that nothing else mattered more.

Justice placed his hands on her hips and slowly pushed her panties down. She stepped out of her heels as she stepped out of her panties.

"Are you on the pill?" he whispered into her ear, but now she was so caught up in watching Hunter, and then Seno and Mace got undressed and she was surrounded by perfection.

Justice gave her a squeeze as he maneuvered his fingers down her belly to her cunt. He stroked between her already wet pussy lips and she moaned.

"Yes. I'm on the pill."

"Good. That means our first time together there won't be any barriers. We want all of you. Every inch, Ellie. No holding back," Justice whispered as he inserted two fingers up into her pussy, while he suckled a sensitive spot on her neck.

Ellie moaned and thrust her breasts forward, feeling them tingle as her nipples hardened. He walked her closer to the bed.

"We want this to be perfect for you, Ellie. Do you trust us to make this perfect?" he asked her and she opened her eyes to find Hunter, Seno, and Mace stroking their cocks and staring at her body.

"This already is perfect. You're all perfect." Her eyes welled up with emotion and Justice removed his fingers and turned her around.

She lay on the bed, and he caressed her thighs open.

"You are one sexy woman, Ellie. Every single inch of you," Hunter whispered as he lay on the bed next to her and stroked a thumb and pointer over her nipple. She inhaled and held his gaze as Seno joined them on the other side.

She looked at Hunter's body as Justice undressed and then moved back between her thighs. Then she looked at Seno who kissed her deeply on the mouth before making his way with his tongue along her throat to her other breast. She grabbed onto his head until Mace took her hand from above her and behind her head. Tilting back, chin lifted so she could see Mace, too, she watched in awe as he sucked her fingers one by one into his mouth, while his brothers suckled her breasts and pussy.

The moment Justice licked between her pussy lips she moaned aloud, feeling her body shake. She felt so incredibly alive and relaxed. She was shocked. There was no fear, only anticipation.

"So delicious," Justice stated as he moved up between her thighs, kissing her belly, her ribs, and then her lips.

"She looks delicious," Seno added, pressing fingers to her cunt while he pulled one nipple between his teeth.

"Oh God, this is incredible."

"You're incredible," Mace told her as he placed her hand over his cock, keeping it covered while he held her gaze. She shivered and a small burst of cream secreted from her cunt.

"She's ready." Mace pulled fingers from her cunt, brought them to his lips, and sucked the glistening cream from them.

She felt her jaw drop and Seno chuckled. "Mace can be very naughty sometimes, Ellie."

"Like you don't want to be naughty with our Ellie?" Mace asked, still licking his fingers before he leaned down and licked her nipple.

"There's plenty of time for that. Are you ready, Ellie? Are you okay?" Justice asked her. She looked toward him, feeling every bit of her about to snap and explode.

"Yes. Please, Justice, make love to me."

"With pleasure." Slowly, he pressed the tip of his cock to her pussy and she closed her eyes. She felt that sense of fear, the bit of anxiety suddenly appear. But then Hunter stroked her cheek.

"Look at him. Open your eyes and see all of us, loving you, caring for you, putting you first."

She did, and the emotions and expressions in their eyes, in Justice's eyes, did her in.

He pressed deeper, easing his thick, hard cock into her pussy stroking, thrusting inch by inch until he filled her.

"Sweet mother, you're tight. Oh God, it's too much." Justice grit his teeth and moaned as he pulled out and then stroked back into her.

"Oh!" She moaned louder and then felt Mace caressing her hair, Seno kissing along her neck and shoulder on the left side, and Hunter on the right. A surge of emotions and feelings consumed her. Their licks and sucks caused chills to erupt over her body. Justice's thick, hard cock felt as if it stretched her inner muscles in a combination of ache and pleasure. It had been so long since she'd had sex. There were so many emotional and physical barriers, yet these four men broke all of them down and gave her the peace of mind, the trust she needed to let them in.

"Oh God, Justice, you're so big. It feels incredible."

Her encouragement seemed to turn him on as he increased his thrusts all while his brothers explored her body and watched him make love to her. She never in her life would have thought that an audience turned her on, but with one this attractive and sexy, she would allow them free access to her whenever they wanted.

Justice began to set a nice pace, grunting and pushing into her pussy, causing her to lose her breath. Her entire body tightened up and then she screamed her release. Justice pulled out and then thrust back into her, fully releasing his seed and moaning her name. He pulled her into his arms and squeezed her tight.

* * * *

Hunter felt that anxious feeling in his gut, yet he also felt a confidence he didn't have with other women. He wasn't so concerned that Ellie would be turned off by his leg, yet he sort of was.

As Justice kissed her one last time and she smiled, she turned to him next. It was like she knew he needed her now. Justice moved out of the way and Hunter eased his body over hers. He cupped her face between his hands and held her gaze. "I could get lost in your eyes, Ellie. They're so green and bright. You're already so special to me. Do you know that?" he asked.

"Why? What do you see in me, Hunter? You're all so perfect and gorgeous. You could have any woman you want, whenever you want."

"Me?"

She snorted as if he were crazy for even thinking he couldn't. "I've seen the way the women look at you, and want you."

"I don't see that. I only see you, Ellie. I see your compassion, your honesty, and your sexy smile, and now this sexy body. I want in."

"Then take me, Hunter. Make me yours."

He smiled and then kissed her as he adjusted his body. Seno and Mace caressed her thighs wider, as Hunter pressed his cock into her cunt.

She grabbed onto his shoulders and then looked down at his legs. He felt that tightness in his chest. That insecurity, that lack of feeling like a true man and then Ellie shocked him. As she counterthrust up into him, she moved her palms along his waist down his sides to his upper thighs and caressed him.

Never, never since losing his leg had a women touched him like this. She held his gaze and tilted her head back as if enjoying and feeling the bond between them so strong just like he was.

"Ellie." He said her name, his voice quivering as he pulled back and then thrust into her holding his cock deep in her cunt.

"Hunter, I'm yours, and you are mine. I feel it," she said, her eyes filled with tears. He leaned forward and kissed her then wrapped his arms around her and thrust into her again and again. Her legs squeezed against his waist and he suckled her neck, licked across her skin, and then lifted up and continued to thrust into her. He felt whole when he was inside of her. Like the man he wanted to be, had been fighting to prove he was, and in this moment, deep inside of Ellie, he felt that man. He felt alive. He caressed along her arms, and raised her arms above her head with their fingers entwined.

Holding her gaze, he smiled as he stroked her pussy in deep, slow thrusts.

"Our Ellie is amazing," he stated. Mace cupped her one breast and Seno cupped the other.

"Her body is a fantasy come true. I can't wait to make love to you, Ellie," Mace whispered and the leaned down and licked her nipple.

"Oh, Mace." She moaned softly and Hunter felt her pussy muscles squeezing his cock.

Seno leaned up and kissed her mouth and then pulled her nipple. She gasped. "I can't wait to fuck you breathless."

"Oh!" She cried out and began to convulse beneath Hunter.

"Fuck, Seno, you got her wild." Hunter thrust two more times and came inside of her. He leaned down and kissed her, and she caressed her hands down his body, over his thighs and then up again.

"Amazing." Hunter kissed her lips before he lifted up and eased his way off of her.

* * * *

Seno pulled Ellie into his arms and on top of him. She lifted up and straddled his waist then reached for his cock. The moment her hands touched his dick he grunted.

"Fuck, you're going to make me come before I even get a chance to feel that tight, wet pussy."

"You're naughty," she whispered, rising up as she held his gaze to align his cock with her cunt.

Mace moved in behind her and caressed her ass.

"I want to get really naughty with this ass," Mace whispered. "Oh God, Mace." She leaned her head back against Mace's chest and Seno chuckled.

"There'll be none of that tonight. She'll need time to get ready for all of us to take her," Hunter reprimanded and Seno raised his eyebrows at her. She blushed.

Seno cupped her breasts and pulled her closer so he could lick the tips. "I think Ellie would love to have a cock in her ass while one is in her cunt and another in her mouth. Isn't that right, Ellie?" Seno asked and then nipped her nipple.

"Yes, oh God, yes," Hunter chuckled.

Mace caressed her ass cheeks and she gasped.

"What's he doing to you, baby?" Seno asked as he reached between them and aligned his cock with her pussy. She slowly lowered down, taking him up into her cunt.

"Touching me."

Seno thrust upward as he held her hips. "Fuck, you're tight."

"Oh, Seno." She gripped his shoulders and closed her eyes, and then she gasped again and shivered.

"What is Mace doing to you now?" he asked and Seno could see Mace over her shoulder. Mace's one hand was on her shoulder pressing her body down as Seno thrust upward. He was doing something behind her and all Seno could imagine was Mace's finger exploring her ass. His own cock hardened. He thrust upward.

"Tell him what I'm doing to you, sweetness," Mace whispered.

"Holy shit," Hunter said from the side and Seno grabbed her hips and thrust up harder, faster.

"Tell him." Justice's command came from the left, but Seno was so caught up in the feel of her pussy muscles gripping his cock as he stroked up and down, he could hardly focus.

"Tell him," Justice repeated and Seno could see Justice next to Mace, his hand caressing her ass and then up her back to her neck and hair.

"Oh God, I can't take it."

"Tell me, Ellie," Seno demanded now, feeling his cock about to explode.

Mace pressed against her.

"He's using his finger, his hands on my ass," she stated breathlessly.

Mace pressed on her back and Seno felt her pussy tighten. "Fuck," he exclaimed as he thrust two more times and then exploded inside of her. Ellie panted against Seno's neck. She licked his skin, sucked on it and pulled.

He wrapped his arms around her and caressed over her ass. Looking over her shoulder as Ellie continued to rock against him, Seno could see Mace's finger in her ass, pumping, stroking her.

Hunter reached over and pinched her ass. "She likes it."

"Hell, she loves it," Justice added and then spanked her ass.

Ellie screamed against Seno's neck and he felt her shaking and coming again.

He ran his hands up her body to her cheeks and cupped them, forcing her to look at him. Her lids were heavy, her lips wet and parted as she moaned and panted.

"Feels good?" he asked, and felt the excitement and desire in his eyes.

"Yes. Oh God, so crazy, but yes."

"Fuck it. I can't wait or I'm going to come all over her back," Mace stated firmly. He gripped onto her hips and lifted her up.

She gasped as Seno moved out from underneath her.

"Oh, Mace," she screamed.

Seno watched along with Hunter and Justice as Mace took her from behind. He watched Mace's dick disappear into her pussy as

Ellie raised up on all fours. She was panting, moaning, and then pushing back.

"Damn, Mace, you got our baby all fired up." Justice cheered him on.

"I think it's our baby that has me all fired up," Mace said through clenched teeth as he thrust in and out of her pussy in fast, deep strokes.

"Oh, Mace. Oh God, you're so big and it feels so tight." She gripped the comforter and pushed back against Mace's cock.

* * * *

Mace never felt so out of control. Ellie had an amazing body, she was gorgeous, sexy, with large breasts and a great ass. The way she accepted Hunter so freely and with all her heart was emotional and automatically gave her a permanent place in his heart, in all of their hearts. He was so scared tonight. He feared she would push them away and instead, here she was trusting them, giving herself to them so freely.

"So good, Ellie. You feel so good."

"More, Mace. I need more, I'm right there, and my arms are shaking."

"Don't you fall down, baby. I'm right there with you." Mace eased his finger over her puckered hole and pressed it through the tight rings of her ass.

She screamed out his name and convulsed underneath him. The sloshing sound filled the room as he continued to thrust into her. He lay over her and wrapped an arm around her breasts, cupping the one on the right and squeezing.

"Mace, oh God, Mace." She slowly fell to the bed and he lifted up so as not to crush her and pulled her legs slightly back off the bed. He lowered and thrust into her, pulling his finger from her ass as he grabbed her hips and continued until he roared and exploded inside of her.

He felt his head spin. He was dizzy, and nearly fell over, but Hunter was there to grip his shoulder. He heard their chuckles.

"Holy fuck, I can't even stand straight," Mace stated aloud. He gently pulled from her body and lay down on the bed, pulling Ellie up into his arms.

He ran his hands along her body, her ass and back, and then to her face as she panted and kissed his chest.

"You got to be illegal, girl. That pussy is lethal."

"Oh God." She moaned and they all chuckled, but Mace held her tight and refused to let go for now. She was their woman, and there was no way he was ever going to let her go. Never.

Chapter 10

"So you're telling me this asshole ex-boyfriend of hers attacked her tonight? Is she okay?" Renaldo asked Luke as they headed into the restaurant site, taking in all the new construction and the details he insisted be changed this morning.

"Are you really still interested in her, when she basically turned you down flat tonight?" Luke asked.

"Of course I am. She doesn't know what she wants. If what you found out is true, she will be perfect for me for quite some time. Think about it. She's was abused, raped, and beaten at knifepoint in her own home. Now, this ex returns to assault her again, probably wants to have sex with her, which leads me to believe she must be good in bed."

"What about the detectives? Our people looked into both of them. What if it's true and they like to share women amongst them and she's theirs? Then what?"

Renaldo shook his head. He didn't want to think about her having sex with a bunch of men. She was too beautiful, too classy and sexy. Plus, he wanted her for himself. When he was done with her, then she could released to one of his clients in exchange for money or valuable art.

"She can't be. And besides, things happen for a reason. Can't you see that? She has no family, no one to worry where she's disappeared to when I take her out of this country."

"And what about the truck that was taken by the cops? They're going to track us down. They're going to question us."

"Calm down, Luke. They cannot attach us to the women and the stolen art. I still have that connection in the police department."

"And you still trust him? We nearly lost everything because of that one asshole who nearly blew the entire operation."

"Did I not get rid of him?"

"You did. But the scare of him destroying this entire operation, and leaking it to the cops was too close for comfort."

"I sure did get rid of him, and no one was any the wiser. And I'll do it again if I have to. If these two detectives get too close, they'll die, too. You're the one who has been insistent upon completing this final deal. You talked me out of running before it gets too hot. We're in this until the end and before long we'll be sitting back relaxing and safe, out of this country set for life. Now just relax yourself and know that the cops don't have shit."

* * * *

Justice answered his cell phone and stepped out of the bedroom. The guys were starting a hot bath for Ellie as her body was beginning to feel sore from the attack.

He closed the door and stood in the hallway in boxers.

"Hey, Vin, what's up?"

"First, how is Ellie? Is she all right? Did that dick hurt her?"

"She's okay. Some bruises and she was really shaken up, but she seems okay around us. Thanks for asking. I'm sorry I didn't head to the gallery with you guys."

"Hey, she's special, and she was in trouble. You belong there. Sam and I have this covered, and Sam called Gunny McCallister, too."

"Gunny? Why? Isn't he working in some special unit for the Texas Rangers?"

"He is, and coincidentally, they've been tracking numerous trucks just like the one the troopers pulled over. Gunny said they have a connection between some stolen artwork that's being imported into the states illegally. Supposedly, from Gunny's investigation, their team of investigators has linked numerous high-profile contributors, to this operation. We're talking embezzlement, prostitution, and recently drugs."

"Drugs? Is Gunny certain?"

"Justice, Gunny said that these routes these people have organized to sneak past the authorities were so good these individuals running the business expanded into prostitution. I've got copies of the files on my laptop. Gunny notified the Feds as well and we're waiting on more information. Get this, Gunny believes that other people have been paid off to turn their heads and allow these trucks and this artwork to make it to their destinations, and the team of investigators believe them to be cops."

"No."

"Yes. Un-fucking-believable to know that some good guys have gone fucking bad. Sam is working with Gunny now to see if there are connections to these women being murdered and any other murder cases in the last several years. They have a list of people who were involved or locked up along the way. There's been a huge investigation taking place right in our own neighborhood for months now."

"Son of a bitch. Well, does it look like Sentinel and Phillips are involved?"

"Well, if they are, they've covered their tracks pretty well. However, Gunny was very interested in the information I provided to him from these murder cases of ours about Sentinel and Phillips's interest in art and women."

"I don't want Ellie near them."

"Um, that's another thing. I mean, she's safe now, she's with you and your brothers, but I need to tell you something."

"What?"

"We looked over the surveillance video at the gallery. There was a delivery, but the video was tampered with. So we didn't actually see what was in the truck besides some pieces of art. Only four, but this was a big tractor-trailer. Anyway, we watched the video, and Sam and I saw Sentinel and Luke with Ellie. They were looking over some art and she was writing things down and taking pictures with her iPad."

"Vin, just fucking spit it out and stop stalling."

"He was all over her. Touching her, whispering in her ear, and she got pissed. She kept pushing him away and although there was no volume, it appeared she was saying she wasn't interested. Now I don't know what he was asking."

"I'll take care of it."

"I'm sure he was just hitting on her and it has nothing to do with—"

"I'll ask her about it and see if it can provide any assistance to what you, Sam, and Gunny have so far."

"Justice, if Sentinel is involved with the art and the illegal prostitution—"

"I get it, Vin. He could have been trying to get her involved or at minimum been trying to get her into bed. I'll fucking handle it."

"Okay. Call me in the morning and I'll bring you up to date."

"I'll be there."

Justice disconnected the call and ran his fingers through his hair. He felt tense, on edge, and angry. How long had Sentinel been hitting on her and trying to seduce her into bed? Why hadn't she told them? Of course she was attacked tonight so maybe she hadn't gotten the chance but what the hell? He was worried. He couldn't let her go back there to her job and be around Sentinel or Phillips. Hell, how was he going to get her to stay away from any man other than him and his brothers? That would be the only way to keep his sanity and lessen his worry to nothing.

"What's going on? Is everything okay?" Hunter asked him as he opened the door.

He looked at his brother. Hunter was in love with Ellie already. He was, too. If he told him and his brothers what was going on and about the investigation, the prostitution, and Sentinel having his eyes on their woman, all hell could break loose.

Hunter closed the door.

"Fucking tell me right now. This has to do with Ellie, too, doesn't it?"

"Damn it, Hunter, just leave it alone for now."

"No. I'm not leaving it alone. You weren't there tonight to see that dick assault her, force his tongue down her throat and touching her, ripping her dress, hitting her. Now tell me."

Justice took a deep breath as the door opened again. This time it was Mace. "What's going on?"

"Tell us," Hunter stated, and Justice looked at Hunter and Mace.

"All right, but try to stay calm and please don't freak out. Ellie has had enough upset tonight, she doesn't need more." Justice explained about the investigation, the phone call from Vin, and about the gallery video.

"That's it. She's done working for him. What if he wants to take her somewhere and sell her off like some sex slave? What the fuck?" Mace said as he began pacing the hallway.

"She didn't even tell us about Sentinel hitting on her. She's keeping secrets," Hunter said, and his expression looked both hurt and angry.

Justice placed his hand on his shoulder. "She couldn't have told us because we didn't talk to her then. When she got to work, Paul attacked her. There was no time."

"But you said they were in his penthouse having lunch and wine a few weeks ago. He's been trying to get her into bed from the start. Hell, look at her body, her personality, and anyone can see she's perfect," Mace added.

"Mace, she hasn't been with anyone in over a year since she was assaulted. We're the first men she's been with."

"What are you going to do?" Hunter asked him.

"I need to talk to her about it. I need to ask her some questions to see if maybe there was something in their conversation that could help our case."

"Well then, let's talk to her," Mace said, opening the door.

"All of us?" Hunter asked.

"No. Just me. You two need to calm down," Justice said and then entered the bedroom. Ellie and Seno weren't there but he could hear them talking. They were in the bathroom.

He walked in just as a very naked, beautiful Ellie was being assisted into the Jacuzzi tub by Seno. She moaned as she got under the warm water, and he felt his cock harden.

"Are you sore, baby?" Justice asked, and both she and Seno turned to look at him. Seno gave a wink and Ellie smiled.

"This feels great. I'm sure after I soak a while I'll feel even better." She leaned back in the tub.

He walked over and sat on the step that led into the big Jacuzzi tub. He glanced at Seno, and Seno squinted his eyes at him then turned toward the doorway. There were Mace and Hunter.

"Ellie, I need to ask you some questions."

"Questions?" she asked him, holding her gaze. She looked so young and pretty. He didn't want her to feel any more fear or pain, but she could help with this investigation if Sentinel really did have a thing for her. He swallowed hard.

"Yes, it's about tonight at the gallery. When you met Sentinel and Phillips there."

Her eyes widened and she swallowed hard and then looked back at the water.

"Ellie, it's okay. Vin saw the surveillance tapes. There may be a connection to the murdered women, the stolen art, and that truck that was at the gallery tonight."

"Really? That's crazy. Venero's is a very prominent gallery."

He reached over and clutched her chin. "How was Sentinel tonight, when you were with him?" He stared into her green eyes and wanted to take the fear away.

"He seemed like himself, why?"

"Does he normally hit on you, stand really close to you, and touch your hair?"

"What?" Seno asked.

She glanced at him and then back at Justice. "What is this about? Why are you asking me this?"

"I need to know what he said to you tonight. Did he make any comments about making you money, taking you to bed?"

"Oh God, no. What are you thinking?" she asked, standing up and reaching for the towel. Seno grabbed and it she pulled it from his hands as Justice watched the water drip from her very large, aroused breasts.

"It's believed that Sentinel and Phillips are involved in stolen art and prostitution. The women who were found murdered had been with either Phillips or Sentinel before they died. An investigative team is making a connection between them and this illegal art and prostitution ring. Sentinel could be either trying the women out, or recruiting them."

She gasped. "And what? You think that he was recruiting me? That I would sell my body for money? That I would allow him or Luke to touch me?" She raised her voice.

"No. Of course not. That's not what I'm asking. I need to know what he said to you and if there was any indication about the art being special or about the women, or something."

She stared at him, holding the red towel around her body and then looked at Hunter and Mace. "He didn't say anything. I don't think he did."

Justice reached for her and she pulled away. He raised his eyes at her and then placed his hands on his hips. "Ellie?"

"No. You know what, I get it. You think I'm weak. You think that I allow men to take advantage of me because I'm scared, don't you?" She was angry and insulted and that wasn't his intention.

"No, of course I don't think that."

"I handled Renaldo coming on to me tonight just like I've handled it from the start."

"What do you mean from the start? This guy has been hitting on you all these weeks?" Seno asked, looking pissed.

"Oh, give me a break. You're a man. You hit on women all the time."

"But we know what the word 'no' means," Mace stated from behind Justice.

"We're losing focus here. This isn't why I asked you about Renaldo." Justice stepped closer.

Ellie stepped back and could go no further but back into the tub. "I handled it."

"How? What did he say and do?" Justice asked.

"He talked about the art and about how he only enjoyed one-of-a-kind, rare pieces. He liked things that people would pay a lot of money for. Things that he could make money off of. He told me that I was gorgeous and classy, that my body was perfect and—"

"And what? What did he say?"

She pulled her bottom lip between her teeth. "He said that he couldn't put a price tag on my beauty. That he would keep me for himself and cater to my every need and desire."

"Asshole," Hunter said from behind them.

"What else?" Justice asked.

"He would take me away, and that he knew I didn't have any family, and I didn't need friends because I would have him. That's when he tried to kiss me."

"Son of a bitch," Seno added.

"Did he? Did he kiss you?" Justice asked.

She squinted her eyes at him and her green eyes filled with anger. "You said Vin saw the video, so why don't you tell me?"

He grabbed her around the waist and hoisted her up into his arms.

She grabbed onto Justice's shoulders as the towel fell from her breasts.

"He didn't say."

She slowly ran her fingers through his hair and held his gaze. "Justice, I may have been a victim of an attack months ago, when I was weak and unknowing, but I'm not the same woman. I got out of the situation with Renaldo when he tried to seduce me into his bed."

Justice bit the inside of his cheek. Just the thought of that fucker touching her and wanting her made his blood boil.

"Even tonight, when Paul attacked, I admit, I was caught off guard, I was scared, petrified, but then I thought of you and your brothers, and wanted to fight, to get back to you and not lose this opportunity to be with you. I don't know what Renaldo's intentions were, but I wasn't biting. I was just trying to get out of there without incident and to get back to you. Don't you trust me?"

"Of course I trust you. You need to trust me, to trust us, so we can keep you safe. I'm worried, Ellie. Somehow you're caught in the middle of this shittin' investigation. I've got beautiful young women, murdered, and a potential suspect is hitting on you, trying to get you in his bed, and I'm a bit fucking angry about it."

She placed her hands against his cheeks and softly smiled, letting her breasts press snugly against his chest.

"Don't be, Justice. I'm here with you. I'm not interested in anyone else except your brothers," she teased. He heard the soft chuckles behind her and he kissed her deeply while she wrapped her legs tightly around his waist as he carried her out of the bathroom.

* * * *

Ellie couldn't believe how commanding and authoritative Justice was. She should be careful to not make him angry, yet because she knew he would never hurt her, she was aroused by his masculinity and the fact he wore a badge for a living. He was sexy, well built, and she wanted him, again.

As Justice laid her down on the bed, he knelt between her legs and gripped the towel in a fist. He used it to lift her and pulled her ass and pussy to the edge of the bed. But he didn't pull the towel away from her body, instead he lowered it so only her breasts were exposed.

Her skin was damp from her bath, and the cool air in the open room made her nipples harden.

He reached down and stroked his thumb along her left nipple, and watched it shrivel up. She parted her lips as he reached for the other nipple and repeated the same action, making an imaginary string from her nipples to her cunt lubricate her pussy.

Reaching into his boxers, he pulled out his cock and stroked the thick muscle while holding her gaze. He was huge, thick, and she wanted to taste him.

"Justice, I want to—"

"Do you now?" he interrupted her, knowing exactly what she wanted to do to him. She felt brazen, alive, and capable of being a seductress and experienced lover for him. She gulped and he softened his intense stare.

"Does sucking on my cock frighten you?" he asked, and she was so touched by his concern. He really was so compassionate.

She shook her head. "I want to. Please?" She lowered her eyes. He stepped closer to her and she reached out and pressed his boxers down his ironclad thighs.

Using her palms, she ran them up and down as he parted his feet to give her better access to his cock and balls. She was shocked at how large he was all over. Being petite, she felt so small and feminine, and it made her want to prove her strength and her ability to be the woman he needed, they needed.

Remembering that they had an audience, she looked to the side and saw them there. Hunter in the single chair, leg up, naked. Mace leaning against the wall with his arms crossed and only wearing boxers, and Seno lying on the edge of the bed on the other side, lounging with his hand holding his head up just staring at her.

She used her hands to cup his balls, and Justice moaned. Glancing up over the thick, hard ridges of stomach muscles toward his massive chest and then his firm expression, she felt her pussy leak.

"What are you thinking right now, my sexy little minx?" he asked her.

She stroked his cock and lowered her mouth to the mushroom top as she used her other hand to touch her pussy under the towel.

"How hard and thick you are. How good you smell, and how hearing you moan makes me wet and horny."

"Holy fucking shit!" Seno exclaimed from behind her. She licked Justice's cock on her last syllable as his eyes widened and then he reached for her.

He pulled the towel from her body and stepped closer as she attempted to take more of him into her mouth. Using her other hand to thrust fingers to her cunt, she became more and more aroused.

"Holy shit, baby, you're fingering yourself?" Mace asked, joining them by the bed. Seno came up behind her on his knees. She could feel his cock against her spine as she bent over to suck Justice with great effort.

"Let me see," Mace said as he maneuvered his fingers over hers, being sure not to touch his brother as she sucked his cock. The moment Mace's thick, masculine fingers touched her cunt and moved inside of her pussy, she moaned.

"Oh shit, that feels incredible," Justice moaned.

"I want in on this action," Mace stated.

"Me, too," Seno said.

"I'll wait and have her all to myself," Hunter chimed in, still sitting in the chair with his leg up.

"Get down on the floor on your knees," Justice told her. She slid down, being sure to not stop sucking and tasting him.

"This is a great ass. Fuckable, actually," Mace said as he spread her thighs, pulled her hips back, and caressed her ass cheeks.

She felt her heart race and wondered if he were going to try anal sex with her. She realized she was so aroused and stimulated that she wanted to.

She pulled her mouth from Justice's cock.

"Mace?"

She hugged Justice's body and sucked the side of his shaft like an ice pop as she caressed his ass and stuck her ass out behind her.

"Yes, sexy?" Mace answered, as he massaged her ass and stroked a finger down the crack.

"I want to try it."

She licked Justice again and then moved her hands along his hard, muscular ass and squeezed it.

"Want to try what?" Mace asked as he leaned against her back. His cock stroked over her pussy lips back and forth as he licked her neck.

"You said my ass was fuckable. I want you to," she whispered, feeling her cheeks warm with embarrassment for asking to get fucked in the ass like this. It was insane.

Justice grabbed her face, stopping her from licking him.

"Honey, are you sure? We don't want to hurt you."

She licked her lips. "Isn't that what you want? To all make love to me together?"

"Of course it is."

"I want it. I'm so wet and I need you. All of you."

She felt the cool liquid against her ass and shivered. "What?"

"You don't need to ask me twice, sexy. I'll just get this ass nice and lubed up and we'll give you what you need."

He pressed his finger into her ass, coasting it between the tight rings with ease from the lube. She thrust back against his finger and he added a second digit.

"Oh." She moaned and thrust her own fingers up into her cunt.

"Hot damn, woman, get up on that bed on all fours. Seno, lay down and let her straddle you." Justice was giving orders and soon she was on top of Seno, taking his cock up into her wet pussy. She started riding him, thrusting and rocking her hips to reach that itch deep inside of her when she felt the hand to her cheek caressing her jaw.

"Forgetting something?" Justice asked, stroking his cock. She smiled and opened for him, bending to the left to accommodate him.

Behind her Mace added more lube and Hunter ran the palms of his hands over her ass cheeks.

"You look gorgeous, lover," Hunter told her. She pressed her ass back against Mace's fingers as she sucked Justice and Seno thrust up into her cunt.

"Okay, baby, here I come," Mace whispered and kissed her shoulder. He pulled his fingers from her ass and she immediately felt the loss. She moaned, almost whimpered, against Justice's cock until Mace lifted her hips higher, causing Seno to pull a little way out of her cunt, before she felt the tip of Mace's cock push through the tight rings. She shivered and moaned.

"Breathe, princess. Just relax your muscles and let him in," Justice whispered as he caressed her hair and slowly pushed in and out of her mouth. She did as he told her and Mace pushed deeper, grunting, moaning as his fingers dug into her hipbones.

"Oh God, baby, this is incredible to watch. Your ass is sucking Mace's cock right inside where it belongs. You're doing so good," Hunter told her and then caressed her ass and back.

"Damn, Mace," Justice stated.

Ellie felt so aroused and so tight and full she needed to move, to do something to reach the point where that itch could be scratched and she could breathe. She sucked Justice harder, faster, bobbing her head up and down as he grunted and gripped her hair. Seno began to set a pace with Mace up and down, in and out. They were taking turns thrusting into her.

"Fuck, she's so tight. Holy shit, I'm there. I'm fucking there!" Mace yelled out and then gripped her hips and thrust one more time.

"Ellie!" Justice yelled out and came inside her mouth. She swallowed quickly and licked him clean.

Seno grabbed a hold of her hips and thrust up and down as she held on to his shoulders.

She felt Mace pull out of her ass slowly, but before she could protest from the loss of his cock, another bit of lube filled her ass and then another cock.

"Oh!" She moaned louder. Hunter was behind her, caressing her ass cheeks wider as he pushed his thick cock into her ass.

"Oh, Hunter. Oh!" She moaned louder until Seno gently nipped her nipple making her scream. She moaned as the small eruption began inside of her. Cream dripped from her pussy, but she needed more. It was right there, just out of reach.

"More. Oh God, it's there, please don't stop. Don't stop," she ordered.

Hunter smacked her ass and then grabbed her hips and began a speedy rhythm that had impressed his brothers by their chants and rooting voices. Seno didn't want to be outdone as he counterthrust, making her scream as an incredible orgasm shook her entire body and made her collapse to Seno's chest, feeling dizzy. Seno thrust up and called out her name as Hunter did the same behind her, coming and thrusting three more times.

"Sweet mother, you are fucking incredible. I love you, Ellie. I don't care that this is all new. I fucking love you. Do you hear me?" Hunter asked her, caressing her hair from her damp cheeks. She looked at him, eyelids half-closed as she still panted for breath. "I love you, too."

Chapter 11

This wasn't how he planned it. She should be in his arms right now, and even in his bed. He did it all for her. He was losing his patience. No other woman would ever do. He needed her and she belonged to him first. He watched and waited. The cops were starting to figure things out. It took them damn long enough, but they were stupid. They had always been stupid and he was always steps ahead of them.

He pulled the bouquet of daisies from the bag and placed them into the vase. Very soon she would be in his arms. He would prove his love, his devotion, and show her how important she was to him. He just needed to get her away from them.

He felt the anger fill his veins. He could kill them. One by one, and she would be easy to manipulate then. He knew her weaknesses. He studied her. She was perfect for him from the start.

"You will say you love me, and I will show you exactly what love is all about."

* * * *

"I've got bad fucking news," Vin stated as he got off the phone with the jail.

Justice was sitting at the desk going over the files with Sam and Gunny.

"What?"

"That was my friend, Davie. He said that Paul was released on bail twenty minutes ago."

"What?"

"I guess he had a good fucking lawyer and a week in jail was enough time for him to think about what he did wrong. He has a court appearance two weeks from today."

"So in the meantime he's free to go around and fucking harass Ellie again? This is fucking bullshit!" he yelled out, causing everyone in the office to look at him.

Sam placed a hand on his shoulder. "Sometimes the system sucks. Just call Ellie at work and let her know. Make sure someone is there to pick her up after work," he told Justice.

"I can't believe this." He texted his brothers and then called Ellie. He wished he were with her right now as he told her. The sound of her shocked voice, the silence, and then her pretending to be brave.

"I'll be fine. You go back to work. I'll let you guys know when I'm done here," she told him and he hung up the phone.

"How did she take it?" Gunny asked.

"Like a fucking trooper. She's scared." He heard the texts go off on his phone and looked down at his brothers' responses. He quickly texted back, and Seno said he would meet her at the office before she left.

"Okay, so when do they want to do this raid on the warehouse?" he asked Gunny.

"Wednesday night. Our sources say a delivery of women and art is coming in. We got the warrants to search Sentinel's and Phillip's homes and offices, plus to bug their phones," Gunny told them.

"We also got another connection to those murdered women. They were hired through a call girl company, half-legit, if you can believe that, which was connected to the manager at Venero's," Sam stated.

"You don't mean Kelly York?" Justice asked. Sam glanced down at the text.

"Yep, that's her."

"Shit, she was so concerned over Tiffany. She was playing us," Justice stated.

"Well, then maybe we ought to go have another chat with her?" Vin suggested.

"Sounds good. Let's go," Justice said, and then Gunny and Sam gathered their things to head out and assist with the raid set up for Wednesday.

* * * *

"So, how are things with you guys and Ellie? Making progress?" Vin asked as they headed out of the department toward the unmarked police cruiser.

Justice got into the driver side and started the engine. "Really good. Honestly, it's incredible."

"You sound shocked, Justice." Vin chuckled.

"Well, I guess I sort of am still in shock. We wanted this—me, Hunter, Seno, and Mace—for so long. We went through some stupid shit with stupid women. Especially Hunter."

"You mean because of his issues about his leg? Man, he's come so far, and has accomplished so very much. He's a role model for other soldiers, other amputees."

"You don't have to tell me. I thought he was doing all right, until Ray Ann."

"Ah hell, that bitch is a conniving two-faced witch. What she said that night at Casper's was frigged up."

"It's funny you bring that up because that's when I saw a change again in Hunter. We had just met Ellie."

"That's right. Sam was with Moira and Ellie. So what do you mean that you saw Hunter change?"

"He was angry, but he was also hurt even if he didn't say so. The four of us are close, and if one is not on his game or has something on their mind, the others just know. It's crazy. But meeting Ellie that night, hearing her stand up for Hunter, not even knowing him, was incredible and showed such character. From there on out, meeting her in other places, trying to get to know her, became a combined effort. We were all on board. We all were attracted to her."

"Shit, I remember your face when she came out of the back room at Tratorra's with Phillips and Sentinel. Holy shit, I thought you were going to do something stupid."

Justice chuckled. "I almost did. But then you guys had the party after Hunter's race, and things just happened naturally between us and Ellie."

Justice was quiet a few moments as they drove down the highway.

"She's been through a lot. It really fucking pisses me off to know that Paul is out there somewhere, free to roam the streets and maybe even be dick enough to try and hurt her again. How the hell are we going to handle this, Vin? What if something happens to her? What if one of us gets there too late if he tries to hurt her again? I love her. We all do."

"I understand your fears, and rightfully so, after everything that has happened. But you can't smother her. You can't constantly be with her even though having her in your arms gives you the peace of mind you need."

Justice looked at Vin and then back at the road. "You get it, don't you? You feel the same way about Moira?"

Vin thought about it a moment. He and his brothers had their own issues that held them back from accepting their feelings for Moira. Link had a bad relationship with a woman he adored who cheated on him, and Sam was a workaholic who never dated.

"I can see myself feeling the same thing, but I'm not sure it's going to work out."

"Why not? Don't Sam and Link care for Moira, too?"

"Sam hasn't spent much time with her, and he's always working or coming up with an excuse to leave. Link has put up a wall since his ex cheated on him. Moira and I haven't even kissed."

"What?"

"I'm serious. I feel like such a dick because she's given me numerous opportunities to kiss her, and I wanted to kiss her, but then I thought about my brothers and I can't make that next step without them. It wouldn't be fair to them."

"What about to Moira? Your brothers may eventually come around as they spend more time with her and let down their guards. Moira could give up on you guys completely if you keep hurting her like that."

"I know. Believe me I know that I'm pushing her away, but I need my brothers on board with this. It's what we discussed years ago, and what we ultimately want, but I just can't get through to them when Link is in pain, and fears rejection and Sam is scared of opening up his heart and providing for a woman. They have trust issues. We all do."

"Well, don't give up on them or on Moira. She's perfect for you guys. If they can see that, and the four of you can come together and take a chance, then maybe Link will open himself up again and Sam will be on board too.

Just then Vin's cell rang. "It's Sam." He answered the call. "Say that again?"

Vin looked at Justice.

"What is it? What's wrong?"

"Kelly York is dead."

Justice slammed his hand down on the steering wheel. "Where? At the gallery?"

"Yes, one of the delivery guys walked into the back storage room and found her. Her throat was slit." He told him and then told Sam they were almost there. Sam said he would meet them there.

Vin disconnected the call. "I have a bad feeling about this."

"So do I. Someone wanted her dead before we had a chance to talk with her."

"Let's hope whoever killed her screwed up and we can get some footage off the security cameras."

"That's right. Maybe the killer didn't know about those," Justice stated as they approached the entrance to the gallery spotting all the police cars and special crime scene unit.

"We're getting close in this investigation, and someone is trying to cover their tracks. This is going to help us nail them, I just know it."

"I hope you're right. Too many people are dying."

* * * *

"Kelly's dead. What the fuck is going on, Renaldo?" Luke asked as he ran his fingers through his hair and paced the inside of the new office at the restaurant.

"We need to get out of here. It's obvious that someone is onto our entire operation. I'm not going down," Renaldo said as he looked down at the desk and started grabbing some things he needed. "Not after all these years of creating this gold mine. Call the airport and get the jet fueled up before the fucking cops arrive and lock us up."

He heard the gunshots and jumped backward looking up, seeing the hole in Luke's forehead between Luke's eyes before Luke fell to the rug.

"You?" Renaldo asked as the shooter came into view, his gun pointed right at Renaldo.

"You're a greedy fuck, and you crossed the line."

"What? How? You got your pay. Why the fuck would you do this? Everything was working out perfectly."

"It's not perfect. When I have her, it will be perfect."

The shot rang out, and Renaldo fell back into the chair in shock.

* * * *

It was late and Ellie was on the phone with Unc.

"Are you sure one of them is going to pick you up from work? I can be there in ten minutes."

"Yes, Unc, Hunter and Seno are on their way. I just can't believe this entire mess is happening. Luke was shot and killed in the office at the new restaurant this afternoon and Renaldo is missing. It's so crazy."

"I told you that Renaldo Sentinel was bad news. I didn't like the fact that you were working for him either. His reputation on the streets says it all."

"I know, Unc. As much as I disliked him hitting on me, and trying to get me to go out with him, he was still very charismatic, and his love for art was impressive. To think that he's involved with the illegal prostitution ring and the stolen art is shocking."

"Not from my perspective. He's a greedy bastard and someone finally gave him what he deserved."

Ellie wasn't surprised by Unc's dislike of the man. Being a retired cop, Unc didn't have much patience for the criminal element. Her uncle Brian hadn't either. The way he died in some convenience store robbery was crazy. They never found the shooter, but the two other men were found weeks later dead in what the police thought was a shooting war. She took a deep breath and released it.

"Text me when they get there. Are they taking you home?"

"No, I packed a bag this morning. I'll be going to their place, and then I have an early meeting tomorrow to close out this project. You know what's really crazy? The realtor who posted the restaurant, which is still under construction, has received over a dozen calls about buying it. No one can do anything until Renaldo is found dead or alive."

"Who even cares? Just cut your ties with this whole thing and move on. I really wish you had a less dangerous job, Ellie."

"I'm in advertising, marketing, and designing. How less dangerous of a job can this be?" She laughed.

"You should consider coming to Ray Ray's and working with me. Maybe you and I can open up our own place?"

She leaned back in her chair and smiled. "That was your and Uncle Brian's dream. It would have been nice."

"We could still make it a reality. Our dream."

She heard the sadness in his voice. “So much has changed, Unc. Meeting Justice, Hunter, Mace, and Seno and surviving being attacked by Paul have put life into perspective.”

“And?”

“And, I love them. I want to have a future with them. They’re good men, Unc.”

“I wouldn’t know. You haven’t exactly introduced them to me. You’ve only told me about them over a week ago at the bar.”

“I’m sorry. With everything that has been going on and dealing with work, I should have made time to introduce you to them.”

“I am your only family.”

“I know. I’m sorry. Oh, Seno is texting me now. He’s outside with Hunter. They’re on their way up. So I’ll talk to you tomorrow and we can make plans?”

“How about lunch?”

“I’ll have to check with Justice.”

“Why?”

“I think because of the investigation, and because Paul disappeared. They don’t want me going anywhere alone, and I honestly don’t want to either.”

“Well, you’re always safe with me. Remember that. Maybe tell the bodyguards that you’re in good hands.”

She chuckled. “Okay, bye.”

She disconnected the call and grabbed her things. As she was pulling on her coat, the secretary came in. “The florist called and said there was a delivery for you. They’re behind, so they want to deliver it tomorrow. Is that okay?”

She smiled. “Flowers, from who?”

“They didn’t say. I can find out.”

“No, that’s okay. Just have them bring them tomorrow because I’m leaving now.”

“I figured as much. There are two really good-looking men out here that say they’re picking you up.”

She smiled wide. "They sure are."

"You are so lucky. They're gorgeous, Ellie."

"Thank you."

Ellie grabbed her purse and headed out of the office. The moment she saw them she walked into Seno's arms and hugged him.

"Hey, gorgeous. I missed you."

"I missed you, too," she said, and then he kissed her quickly on the lips. Hunter reached out his hand and she gave him hers. He brought it to his lips and kissed the top of her hand as he looked down into her eyes.

"Can't wait to get you home," he stated with promises in his eyes.

She felt her nipples harden and her pussy leak in anticipation. "I can't wait to get home."

They walked out together, hand and hand, with her heart filled with love and with people watching them as they left together. She thought about Unc and how she hadn't introduced the men to him. She suddenly felt guilty and wondered if she had insulted him. Unc had taken good care of her after Uncle Brian died. She loved him. He was such a good friend, and yes, he was family. This family was going to expand with the Lawson men, too, and they all needed to meet him.

"There's someone I want you to meet," she told them and felt instantly better just thinking that they would meet Unc and hopefully Unc would like them. She texted him and then asked Seno and Hunter to head to Ray Ray's.

Chapter 12

"Are you sure, Sam?" Vin asked his brothers as Justice and the other detectives went over the information they had between the coroner's reports, the surveillance videos from both the art gallery and the construction sight of Sentinel's new restaurant.

"It's the same guy, and looking at the height alone, our killer isn't Sentinel. Someone else killed those women, Kelly York, Phillips and now it looks like they took Sentinel with them," Sam told them.

"Shit. What the hell could we have missed? Is there someone else, a higher-up involved with this whole scam that none of us have identified?" Justice asked.

"Justice, we should call Gunner and send this stuff to him immediately. His team has been on this investigation from the start, and trying to take down the mastermind behind the illegal art and the prostitution ring. Maybe the investigators have another lead, a person of interest?" Sam asked.

"Call him. Do it. We don't have anything else," Justice said. Sam pulled out his cell as Vin starting pulling everything they had onto the computer so they could send Gunner all of it. Feeling frustrated and not having anything else to do at the moment, he called Hunter to check on Ellie. They were stopping for dinner before heading to their place.

* * * *

Hunter excused himself from the table to take a call from Justice. He smiled at Ellie as she laughed at something Unc said and Seno smiled. When she had said she wanted them to meet a very important man in her life, it nearly gave him a heart attack. Then she told them all about Unc, Ray Ray's, and her uncle Brian who died in a convenient store robbery gone badly.

"Hey, Justice, what's going on?"

"A lot of crap. This case is hell. How's our girl?" he asked, and Hunter smiled as he leaned against the wall closer to the bar and watched Seno, Ellie, and Unc talking. Then Seno got up and headed toward the men's room.

"She's doing great. We stopped by Ray Ray's. Her good friend Unc works here."

"Unc? Who is that?"

"Apparently like a father to her. I guess this is the man we need to impress in order to get his good wishes for us to be with Ellie."

Justice chuckled. "That serious, huh?"

Hunter turned toward the doorway as he spoke. "He's a nice guy, but definitely protective of Ellie. We're learning a lot about her, and her uncle Brian who was killed in a robbery. She really has gone through a lot, Justice. I want to keep her safe, and help her to be happy."

"I want that, too. Give her a kiss for me and maybe I'll see you later tonight."

"You may not come home?" Hunter asked.

"I'll try my hardest, but there's a killer out there, and before he strikes again, we need to figure out who he is."

"Well, be safe. Hope to see you later. Bye."

* * * *

"So what do you think of Hunter and Seno?" Ellie asked Unc. He held her gaze and he looked unsure.

"I hate to say it, but they're nice. They're also big guys filled with muscles, so I suppose they'll keep you safe."

She smiled. "All four of them are big guys with muscles, Unc." She took a sip of her wine.

"When do I get to meet the other two?" he asked.

"Well, Justice is working with some other detectives and, I think, the Feds in regards to the murder investigation."

"Feds?" he asked.

"Yeah, it's pretty intense. I worry about him. This person who has killed these women, and apparently Luke Phillips, may have Renaldo. Hunter just told me about it on the way over here."

"Well, thank goodness you weren't with Sentinel when this person attacked. You could have been killed."

"I know. It's scary. But I'm safe, Unc," she told him, covering his hand with hers.

"You sure are. I'll protect you and be here for you like always." She smiled as Hunter returned.

"Important call?" she asked.

"It was Justice. He said hello."

"Oh, is he coming here?"

"No, he's going to be working late. He sends his love, oh, and a kiss from him to you." Hunter leaned over and kissed her softly on the lips. Unc squeezed her hand and let go. She blushed as Seno came back.

"Are you guys just about ready to go? Mace said he'll be home in fifteen minutes from work."

"Great."

"You're leaving so soon?" Unc asked.

"We'll come back another time. We'll bring Justice and Mace so you can meet them, too," Ellie said and then stood up.

Unc gave her a hug and a kiss and then shook Hunter's and Seno's hands.

"You take good care of her. Or else."

She chuckled, but Hunter and Seno held Unc's gaze a moment before they escorted her out of the restaurant.

"So Unc is kind of intense, huh?" Seno asked her as he opened the passenger side door of the truck and helped her hop up into the cab. He was sure to caress his palm over her ass as she got in.

"Intense? No, not really. Did he seem intense?" she asked.

"Only when he threatened us before we just left," Hunter stated and then chuckled as he got into the driver side of the truck.

"Well, he's the only semifamily I have left. He and Uncle Brian were best friends. They were partners before retiring from the police department. I think he's extra protective of me since Uncle Brian died because he felt obligated to care for me. He felt like he failed Uncle Brian because he wasn't there to protect him. The three of us did a lot of things together. I had no one. No family except for Uncle Brian and Unc, so when he died, it was devastating for both of us. We helped one another get through it, and he's been my rock. I owe him so much."

"He was there for you after Paul attacked you that night?"

"He never liked Paul. He thought he was all wrong for me, but he was supportive in my decision. He never said I told you so after Paul assaulted me. Instead, he took care of me. I thought I insulted him today, by not letting him meet the four of you sooner. I'm so glad that he at least met both of you."

"We're glad to have met him as well," Hunter stated.

"Yes, and anyone who has good intentions and means to protect you is all right in my book. I'm sure we'll all become friends soon enough," Seno added.

"Me, too." She hugged his shoulder.

* * * *

Mace was in the shower when he heard bathroom door open. "Hey, beautiful," he called out as he watched Seno help Ellie undress.

"Hi."

He watched Seno cup her breasts from behind and then smooth his palm down her belly to her cunt. She reached up and back, to touch

Seno's cheeks with her hands, and the move caused her large breasts to push forward.

"Oh." She moaned as Seno inserted fingers to her cunt.

"You're so sexy, Ellie. I love this body," Seno whispered. She turned her head to kiss him while he continued to thrust fingers up into her pussy.

"Fuck, baby, I can't wait. Sorry, Mace," Seno said. He pulled his fingers from her pussy, lifted her up, and placed her onto the vanity. They were a few feet away from the shower, but Mace had a perfect view as Seno shoved his pants down, stepped out of them, and then parted Ellie's thighs. She grabbed onto his head and then his shoulders as Seno cupped her ass cheeks and thrust into her to the hilt.

They all moaned. Seno held himself within her, and Ellie squeezed her thighs and calves up against Seno's waist. Mace could see the definition and tone of her calves and thighs as she pressed against Seno.

"Fuck, I'm home. Inside you, I'm home, baby," Seno told her then pulled out and thrust back into her. He repeated the motion, moving faster, shaking the vanity as their bodies slapped against one another. It was so erotic Mace felt his cock harden. He reached down and rubbed his shaft, wanting, needing to be inside of Ellie, too.

"Oh, Ellie. So fucking tight. Damn, baby, I need more."

He pulled out, lifted her up, and turned her around. "Grab the vanity." She did, and with her tits swaying, her full round ass lifted toward Seno, she looked like a sex goddess.

Smack.

Seno spanked her ass and she screamed. "Oh, Seno."

He grabbed a hold of her hips and shoved his cock into her pussy from behind. Mace watched, getting fully turned on. His need, his desire to join in and have her, became impossible to ignore.

"That's so fucking hot. Holy shit, I need her next," Mace stated.

"Oh!" Ellie screamed her release, and Seno cupped her breasts from under her arms and rocked into her three more times before he exploded inside of her.

He could see Seno's legs shaking, and his brother laid his cheek against her neck and shoulder. "Hell, baby, you are my everything." Seno kissed her shoulder and then slowly pulled from her body.

"Bring her to me. Now," Mace commanded.

Seno chuckled as he massaged Ellie's shoulders and walked her toward Mace.

"I need you."

She smiled at Mace as she opened her arms and let him lift her up and against him.

Mace pressed her against the tile wall. He held her gaze and she looked so sexy. Her eyes glistened with desire and satisfaction.

"Ready?" he asked, breathing heavy, anticipating penetrating her pussy and finding relief and satisfaction in being where he loved most. Inside of Ellie, lost in bliss.

"Yes." She shocked him when she reached between them, aligned his cock with her pussy, and slowly eased down over his sensitive shaft.

"Oh." They both moaned together as he penetrated her fully. They remained like that, still, not moving for a few moments, but it became too much for Mace. He kissed her with vigor, exploring her mouth with his tongue and teeth. He ate at her, devoured her scent, her taste, everything about his woman.

"I love you, baby." He pulled back and shoved into her.

"Oh, Mace, I love you, too." She panted as he continued to set a faster pace. His dick never felt so hard, so ready to explode. The sight of her mouth, her luscious breasts moving, swaying with every thrust made him grunt and stare at her with such hunger and need.

"I love fucking you."

She chuckled and then shoved down harder, countering his thrusts. "I love getting fucked by you," she replied. He gripped her hair and head then covered her mouth in a lethal kiss that would mark her as his own. He thrust and thrust, stroking her pussy until she pulled her mouth from his and screamed her release.

"Oh fuck, baby. I don't want to come. I fucking don't want to." He thrust and held himself within her as he lost the fight to keep making love to his woman. She felt too damn good, too tight and perfect. He loved her so much. He would die without her. "You're my everything," he confessed. She wrapped her arms around his neck and kissed him gingerly. She kissed his lips, his cheeks, his chin, and then his neck before going back to his lips.

She whispered, "You mean everything to me, too."

* * * *

Hunter waited not so patiently on the bed. He was staring at his leg, the stump where his knee should be and then his shin, calf, and foot. His thighs were super muscular. Absolutely perfect like some Olympic competitor. Yet still, he felt as if he weren't good enough.

"Hey, soldier." He looked up to see Ellie, totally naked, and making her way toward the bed. His eyes fixated on her breasts, the tight, pink nipples and her blotchy chest. She was trying to be sexy and seductive. To put on a courageous act but he knew she was sweet and innocent. It gave him great pleasure and instantly aroused his cock to see her like this. To watch her with hunger in her eyes.

"Come lie down. I need you." She shook her head as she crawled on all fours over to him. Her breasts swayed, her thighs parted, revealing her glistening cream. She licked her lips and leaned forward to lick his lips before she kissed him seductively. As she plunged her tongue into his mouth and he caressed a hand over her back and ass, she gripped his cock, stroked it, and caressed it firmly.

He pulled from her mouth. "Holy shit, baby. Did my brothers get you all fired up?"

"Maybe." She looked down toward his cock and, of course his leg. He tightened up and gripped her hair. "Lie down and let me make love to you."

"I had something different in mind," she told him.

Like some seductress, she slowly lowered onto the bed down his body and between his thighs. She held his gaze as she lowered between his legs and kissed his left inner thigh, so close to the stump he thought he would shed a tear. She wasn't turned off by it, she didn't cringe or turn away. She licked along his inner thigh as she held his gaze. Her delicate manicured fingers coasted up his crotch to his cock and balls. He held the sheets on the side of his waist.

"Oh fuck, Ellie, what are you doing?"

"Loving you, Hunter. Every inch of you." She ran one hand down along his bad leg and caressed over every inch of it. Then she did the same thing to the right before she lifted up onto her knees and presented herself to him.

She reached for his hands and brought one to her breast for him to cup and play with. Of course he did immediately. Loving the fullness, the femininity in his hand and the pleasure he gave her. She shocked him again when she pulled his other hand down, pressed her finger over his pointer and then directed it toward her pussy. She thrust both their fingers up into her as she closed her eyes and moaned.

"Holy shit, Ellie."

"Holy shit, Ellie, is right." Justice entered the room and she didn't even look at him, but Hunter felt her gasp.

"Touch me while I make love to you," she whispered with her eyes open and love shining strong.

"Ellie, you don't have to be on top."

She pressed a finger over his lips. "I want you. I want to try this, so shut up and let me." He was shocked, but also incredibly aroused. His brothers chuckled but he didn't care one bit as Ellie pushed his fingers away from her cunt and replaced them with his cock. She lifted up and lowered down, the whole thing making him harder than a steel rod.

Up and down she thrust on top of him, holding his shoulders, and rubbing her breasts closer to his face. He would stick his tongue out to take a taste or grab one and pull making her pussy wetter, slicker with every stroke. He grabbed her hips and started thrusting upward, both of them moaning and trying to reach fulfillment.

"I love you, Ellie. I love you so fucking much," he told her.

She leaned down and kissed him. "I love you, too, Hunter. You feel incredible. I feel so full," she stated.

"You're about to feel fuller, honey." Justice stated over her shoulder, caressing her back as he gripped her hair and fisted it. She smiled up at him.

"You want to join in?" she asked, all sassy.

Justice's eyes darkened. "Hell yeah, woman," he replied.

She looked at Hunter, and ran her hands up and down his pectoral muscles while she continued to grind her hips, and pussy over him. "Can he join us, Hunter?"

Hunter used his hands to caress over her ass cheeks and part them. "Fuck yeah. I can't wait to see what your face looks like when you have a cock deep in your ass."

"Oh God." She closed her eyes and moaned. He felt her release more cream.

They all scooted down to the edge of the bed, and Hunter lay his legs over the edge as Justice moved in behind her.

"I missed you, sweetness," Justice told her as he kissed down her spine.

"I missed you, too."

* * * *

Justice was so relieved to stop home for a few hours and see his brothers and Ellie. To walk in on her fucking Hunter, and loving him the way she was, filled his heart with adoration and joy. No woman ever made any of them feel so special. He would do anything for Ellie. Hell, he'd die for her.

He grabbed the lube and pressed some to her ass, making her shiver. Stepping into position behind her, he stroked a finger between her ass cheeks and moved the lube around.

"I love this ass. Are you ready for me, baby?"

"Always, Justice. I love you," she told him just as he pressed the tip of his cock to her anus.

He paused, and leaned forward against her back, letting his thick, hard cock slide in as he held her still. "I love you, too," he whispered into her hair, as she panted and tried to pull forward. He shoved all the way in and she relaxed in his embrace.

"I'm in, lover," he told her. Hunter thrust up and then out, so Justice pulled out and thrust in. As they began to set a rhythm, Ellie reached back to hold on to Justice while also reaching forward with her other hand to hold on to Hunter.

Justice sucked her neck with every stroke, making her shake and shiver. Hunter cried out his release and then Justice and Ellie continued to counterthrust. In and out his dick slid, her pussy muscles gripped him tight, and his cock grew thicker.

"Oh, Justice. Oh God, you're too big." She shook from her release.

"Never too big for the woman who's meant to be mine." He thrust two more times, held himself within her, and came. As she lay forward and kissed Hunter, Justice could see the love, the passion and contentedness, in his brother's eyes, and he felt his own eyes tear up.

God, I love this woman. Please let us have happiness like this forever. Never let her leave. Never let anything tear us apart.

Chapter 13

Ellie was in her office working on getting a new client when her cell phone rang. She answered it.

"Hi, Moira. What's going on?"

"Well, you tell me. I was wondering how everything was going with the Lawson men. I heard through the grapevine that you've been spending lots of time with them."

She chuckled.

"You know I have been. I think I've stayed at their place enough this week alone, don't you think?"

"That's great. I'm so happy for you. They're good men."

"I know they are. I rally car for them."

"I'm happy for you. So when are we all going on a girl's night out? Donella and Jessie want to know too."

"Hmmm, I guess I'll have more time once I wrap up this project at work. I'll call you, or see you later at the house."

"No, you won't. You'll be wrapped around one of your men by the time you're out of work, and probably spending another night in their big, muscular arms," Moira teased.

"You're probably right."

"You lucky girl. Call me."

"No problem. Bye."

Just as she put the cell phone back down onto her desk, she saw that it was Seno and she smiled. What a hell of a night they all had last night. She had shown them a side of her she never knew existed until they came along. She loved them so much.

"Hey, Seno, how are you?" she asked.

"Good, baby. How are you? A little sore?" he teased. All because when she got up this morning she was a bit achy and kind of slow moving. But after a shower and some coffee then some kissing from her men, she was as good as gold. The only negative part was that Justice hadn't been there. He got a call about four in the morning and headed to the department.

"Nope. Ready for round two in about five hours," she said, noticing that it was nearly one o'clock.

"Have you eaten lunch yet?"

"Nope, why are you asking? Are you going to come by with something?"

"Actually, I got a call from Unc. He asked if it was okay if he picked you up for lunch today. He knows that we're all taking extra precautions to keep you safe. We exchanged numbers last night at Ray Ray's."

"That's great. I'm so glad he did that. I told you guys that he's a good man, and really cares about me."

"I know he does. That was quite obvious yesterday. Anyway, of course we said it was fine, but we just want you to text us and let us know everything is okay. I know he's retired law enforcement, but we still worry."

"Not a problem. When will he be—"

She started to ask what time Unc was coming when she saw him talking with Lionel as they walked into the main office. Lionel loved bullshitting with Unc. It was the whole law-enforcement thing.

"He's here now. I'll talk to you later."

"Okay. Have fun. Love you, baby."

"Love you, too," she said as Unc walked in.

"Was that Seno?"

"Yes, he told me that you called him." She stood up, straightened out her skirt and blouse, and then reached for her purse placing the cell phone inside of it.

"I hope you don't mind. We exchanged numbers yesterday."

"Of course not. I'm glad you called him. So where are we going?"

"I have this new place a little ways outside of the county. It's fairly new. Opened up two weeks ago, but supposedly has a great steak over salad for you, of course, and a nice porterhouse for me."

"Hmm, sounds delicious. Let's go."

They headed outside and got into Unc's truck.

"You look very pretty by the way. You're practically glowing today."

She felt her cheeks warm and smiled. "Thanks, Unc. I'm very happy."

"You're really in love with four men?" he asked, sounding almost disappointed and disgusted. She looked at him.

"I love them, and it feels right."

He held her gaze and without a word placed the truck into drive and off they went. She didn't know why, but she felt as if Unc was still having difficulty accepting her decision of having a ménage relationship with the men. Why was he being so stubborn? He wasn't that old, only in his early fifties. He looked a lot younger and was in great physical condition. But he was definitely having a hard time with this. What could she do to ease his mind?

"You seem upset, Unc. Is it that you're worried that Justice, Mace, Seno, and Hunter could turn out like Paul?"

"I didn't like Paul from the start. You were too good for him. Too beautiful and innocent. He corrupted you, and I'm afraid that these men will do even worse."

"Unc, how could you say that? You met Seno and Hunter. You said you liked them."

"What was I to say? Hunter isn't even whole. He's not even a real man. Seno, shit, he didn't even give me a hard time about taking you to lunch. How does he know that I don't have feelings for you? What if I did? He'd let just any guy take you to lunch? You know why he didn't care, don't you, Ellie?" he asked her, sounding very different than the Unc she knew.

"Why?" she whispered.

"Because they already had sex with you. They can get it any time they want."

She gasped. "Stop the truck!" she yelled at him and reached for the door.

"That's not the plan, Ellie. I've worked too hard all these years. I waited all this time to have you, and now these four fuck heads that don't deserve you show up and whisk you away? Not fucking happening."

"Oh God, are you out of your mind? What would Uncle Brian say? You were his best friend. Why would you say such hurtful things to me right now?"

"Hurtful? You think this is hurtful?" he yelled at her as he pulled the truck off to the side of the road.

He grabbed her hair and yanked her closer.

"Hurtful is watching other men fuck you when you belong to me. You're never going to see them again. They're finished. The plan is in motion. I'm going to prove to you once and for all that I'm the man for you. I'm the one who has stood by your side all these years. I was there when Paul attacked you. I did everything in my power to protect you until you would finally realize that you and I belong together."

She shook her head and tried to get out of the truck. "You're sick. You lost your mind." She grabbed for the handle of the door just as the needle stuck her neck. She covered her neck where he stuck her.

"Sorry, sweetie, but I can't lose you. Everything I did, I did for you, for us."

She instantly started to feel the effects. Whatever he gave her, it was strong. She saw double of him, triple, and he smiled as he cupped her cheek.

"I'm going to take good care of you, Ellie. Like always. We're going to finally be together tonight." He held her against his side and cupped her breast as he kissed her until darkness overtook her vision.

* * * *

"Oh God, are you seeing this?" Sam asked Vin as they looked over the information Gunner was sending them from the Feds.

Vin looked at Sam. "Ellie."

"I know. Holy shit."

"What's going on?" Justice asked as he walked into the room, closing up his cell phone.

"Justice, Gunner just sent us this information. You know how the investigation was leading the Feds to believe that law enforcement or government employees may have been aiding in the prostitution ring?"

"Yes."

"Well, turns out that a report was filed, unofficially with the police department. It never made it past the lieutenant in charge because that lieutenant is one of the names on the list the Feds have as possible suspects. Now as they dug further, and the Feds were able to pull the prints from Sentinel's office, they came back as matching a retired cop's"

"Who is it?"

"A guy by the name Ray Wallace."

"Ray Wallace? I don't know anyone by that name."

"He works at a local bar, Ray Ray's."

"Ray Ray's?" Justice asked.

"Justice, the Feds are there now, it's Unc. Ellie's family friend," Vin stated.

"Oh shit," Justice said and then pulled out his cell phone.

"What is it?"

"I just got off the phone with Seno. Unc called him to let him know he was taking Ellie to lunch. He has Ellie with him."

* * * *

"I'm not understanding any of this," Seno stated, and Justice drove the truck as they listened to what he had to tell them.

"Okay, so this whole prostitution thing has been going on for over ten years. Gunner and the team of Feds have been pulling in people, questioning them, and getting confessions for lesser charges. It seems that Phillips and Sentinel were the masterminds behind this. But they needed help from law enforcement, border patrol, and others in order to get these shipments across borders and through checkpoints. They greased a lot of hands including some law enforcement. Ellie's friend Unc worked under that Lieutenant and a few others who have now confessed to helping in this smuggling trade all along. As the Feds uncovered in the last twenty-four hours, Unc had been playing a major role in this process. He's our main killer. It has to be him."

"How do you know, Justice?" Seno asked.

"He used his old police revolver to kill Phillips. They were able to trace the bullet to the type of gun used. That gun was confiscated from Unc's desk drawer by the Feds when they went to arrest him. I'm waiting for more details and evidence, but he definitely seems to fit the bill."

"Shit, and I let him have her. What does he want with Ellie?" Seno asked.

"She's the only family he has, maybe he knows he's about to get busted and he's trying to take off and wants her with him," Hunter said.

"Ellie wouldn't go. When Ellie realizes that Unc is the killer we've been searching for, she's going to lose it," Justice told them.

"Unless he means to do her harm, too," Mace told them.

"What do you mean? Why would he want to hurt her?" Seno asked. "She means so much to him."

"I never met the guy, but you two did. You said he threatened you."

"That was typical parental talk. He was there after Paul assaulted her. He was there long before that when her uncle was alive," Hunter added.

"Her uncle? You mean the Uncle Brian she told us a little about?" Justice asked as they pulled into the parking lot. They were meeting everyone there. The Feds and all local police departments put out a description of Ellie and Unc as well as Unc's vehicle. Gunner had someone looking at property ownership or any other homes, condos or even cabins around the state that Unc might have owned or stayed at. The Feds already notified the airports, train stations, and bus lines, and the media was posting Ellie's picture during all broadcasts.

"What are you thinking, Justice? You don't believe that her uncle Brian had anything to do with this, too, do ya?" Hunter asked.

They all got out of the truck and made their way across the media line, dodging questions, and then ducked under the yellow danger tape.

"Justice, the Feds have a team at Ray Wallace's place. You're not going to believe what we they found on his computer in his basement. He had a hidden room in the back cellar. The K-9 sniffed it out and the Feds broke in and gathered everything. It's all right there. The entire operation, details, schedules of deliveries, and—"

Sam looked at Vin and then at Justice and his brothers. One of the Federal agents was standing there as well.

"What else? What is it?" Justice asked.

"There were pictures of Ellie, Justice."

"Okay, so he was her family, why wouldn't he have pictures?" Hunter asked.

"Not those kind of pictures. Some were of her in her bikini by some pool, others were her walking into work, hanging out with friends, and then there were ones he superimposed into other bodies."

"What does that mean?" Mace asked.

"Oh shit, and I let him have her. I handed her right over to a man obsessed with her in that way. Oh God, he's going to hurt her. He's going to kill her. Fuck!" Seno yelled out.

Mace and Hunter placed hands on his shoulder.

"How about a location of a hideaway? Anything come up?" Justice asked Vin and Sam.

"They're going over everything in the room. He's obsessed with her, so maybe he won't actually hurt her. As long as she cooperates with him, it will buy us the time to locate her," Vin added.

"If he's obsessed with her, has been stalking her, and he knows about the four of us, he may just punish her for that and then kill her," Seno stated.

"We can't think that way. They have a lot of documentation to go over. More help is headed to Wallace's place. They'll find something."

"Oh, how about looking into Ellie's Uncle Brian? He died in a robbery or something over a year ago. He was a cop, too," Justice told Sam.

"Brian? Brian what?" Sam asked,

"Brian Morrison, just like Ellie. He was her father's brother."

Sam pulled out his cell phone.

"Yeah, listen, on that list of the murders you were making a connection to, was there a Brian Morrison?"

"Okay, if you don't mind looking into that it would be great. Thanks."

Sam disconnected the call.

"I have someone checking into that. Do you think her uncle could have been part of this and just had bad luck to get killed in the robbery?" Sam asked.

"Not sure. It may have nothing to do with this case. The only reason Ellie is in the middle of it is because her uncle's best friend, our killer, is obsessed with her. We have to find her quickly," Justice added.

"We will. Someone was bound to see them before sundown," Vin added.

* * * *

Unc walked around the bed and watched her sleeping. He had undressed her, and placed her in a very special negligee he had picked out for her in yellow. It had pretty little daisies along the bodice and one more on the sheer pale yellow panties. She looked so beautiful. Her body was perfect, her breasts full and round. He had waited so long for this moment that he hardly could concentrate on anything else.

He had made a mistake in the amount of drugs he had injected her with. So she slept all night, which made it easy to dress her and to get the room ready. The cabin was small, and he had to hide her presents in the other tiny bedroom, but he would bring them to her, and show her how much he cared.

He ran a hand along the white comforter and then walked over toward the window. No one would find them out here. It was miles into the woods out in the middle of nowhere. There were no small towns to drive through, so no one had seen him arrive late last night. It wasn't registered under him, but under Brian with Ellie as the sole owner. She didn't even know. Out here they could expand this house, and do anything to it that she wanted to do. Anything that would make her happy.

"Sleep, my little lover. When you wake, we have some celebrating to do."

* * * *

"We got something!" Sam yelled out and everyone looked up from their laptops and waited.

"Gunner is on the line. They located a cabin four hours from here that was listed under Brian's name with Ellie as a co-owner. It has to be the location he took her."

"Do they have a plan? It's fucking three o'clock in the morning, how are we going to find it and get to her in time?" Justice asked.

Sam held up his finger. "Okay. Yes, they'll be ready. Thanks."

He disconnected the call.

"The Feds have satellite images of the place. They're working on getting details of how many people may be inside and where they can land a couple of choppers at a far enough distance to not tip Wallace off that we're coming," Sam told them.

Justice looked at his brothers. They were all exhausted, scared, and thinking the worse.

"Can we go, too?" Seno asked.

"Gunner said the terrain is difficult, so he's getting gear ready. Let's go wait for our ride," Sam said, and they all headed out of the building.

* * * *

"She loves me, she loves me not. She loves me, she loves me not."

Ellie heard the muffled voice, and felt something tickling her skin. She was sore and felt dizzy. As she tried to open her eyes, the sunlight coming from the window was blinding her. She moved her arms but they wouldn't budge. She was tied to a bed. Then Unc was there, smiling. He was holding daisies in his hand and pulling the petals one at a time. He would drop the petals on her skin. They landed on her belly. She felt the chills and saw what she was wearing. A very skimpy, see-through yellow teddy. She gasped and tried again to get up from the bed.

"She loves me, she loves me not," Unc said as the last petal from the flower landed on her.

She looked at his eyes. The man was long gone. He wasn't sane. She knew that now, a bit too late, but she knew it.

"Unc?"

"Shhhhh. I need more flowers. They're wrong," he stated firmly and stood up.

She moved her legs side to side and tried to lift herself higher up the bed to gain leverage. She didn't want to be lying down with him next to her on a bed. But then, he must have seen her naked. He undressed her and put her in this thing.

"Did you touch me? You didn't, did you?" she asked him, feeling the tears well up in her eyes. He just went about his business as if she weren't even there. Then he came back, sat right next to her, and clutched her thigh. She gasped and tried to pull away, but he dug his fingers into her flesh.

"You need to behave. There's a lot to explain. But first, I have to find the right flower. The one that tells the truth."

He picked up another flower. She saw a whole bunch lying at the bottom of the bed.

"She loves me, she loves me not. She loves me, she loves me not." He just kept pulling the petals, and he must have been at it for a while, because looking down, she saw that the comforter around her frame was covered.

"Unc, why are you doing this? Why?"

He was getting to the final petals. She could see that there were four left. He was going to get the same result again.

"She loves me, she loves me not, she loves me, she loves me not." He slammed the stem onto the ground, stood up and stomped on it.

"No! It's wrong. They're all wrong."

She heard a noise coming from the other room. She looked that way, and he gave her an angry expression and then a smile.

"You think I wouldn't do anything for you, Ellie? I'll show you, and then you'll love me, petals or not."

He started rambling on to her about a prostitution ring, illegal art, and being part of a business venture that made him millions.

"Do you mean you worked for Renaldo?" she asked and he became angry.

"Renaldo is a pussy. He had the world by the balls but he made a huge mistake. His worst mistake ever."

"What was that?"

"He wanted you, and you belong to me."

He opened the bedroom door and dragged what sounded like a chair closer.

She was shocked to see Renaldo. He looked like hell, was bleeding from his shoulder, and could hardly breathe.

"Tell me again that she is mine, not yours. Tell her so she knows what I would do if any other man tries to fuck her."

"Yours. Yours," Renaldo said and then coughed.

She felt the tears roll down her cheeks. Unc was a madman, and she was now tied to a bed and at his command.

"He needs a hospital," she told Unc.

"He's going to die. Just like Paul."

"Paul?" she asked. Unc smiled. He walked back toward the bed and she tried unsuccessfully to get away from him. He grabbed her throat and then held her face as he knelt up onto the bed. His bloodshot eyes trailed over her body.

"He took away your innocence, an innocence that belonged to me, and no one else."

He moved his hand down her throat and cupped her breast.

"Don't, Unc. Please don't do this. Don't hurt me."

His eyes widened. "But I need to hurt you. I need to get them out of your system and make you see only me and what I have done to prove my love. They cannot compare. I have money, I have power, I've killed for you. I even got rid of that pain in the ass uncle of yours."

"What?" she asked, tears flowing and then anger filled her gut.

"You killed him? You killed Uncle Brian?"

He jumped up onto the bed and straddled her waist. He gripped her throat, applying just enough pressure to make her cough and shiver in fear that he could strangle her and kill her.

"He had to die. He stood in the way of my plans."

He released one hand from her throat but kept her in place with the other hand. He slowly moved one palm down between her breasts. He cupped one, and gently ran his thumb over her nipple.

"Oh God, Unc, please don't do this to me," she cried out.

"Brian found out that I was helping Sentinel, so I had to stage that robbery and get him killed. Too many people and families would have suffered. I was just getting ready to retire from all that. I saved a lot of money for us. We could go anywhere you'd like, Ellie. All you have to do is tell me that you love me the way I love you."

"I can't do that. If you loved me, then you wouldn't have killed Uncle Brian."

He jumped up off of her. "That's not true. I told you that he stood in the way of us. Renaldo stood in the way, too. I just wanted him to see us together and realize that you belong to me."

"I don't belong to you."

"Yes, you do. I killed for you. Paul can never hurt you again because of me." He stomped toward the bedroom, disappeared behind the door, and then came back dragging Paul across the floor. There was blood everywhere.

"No! Oh God, no!" she screamed.

Unc dropped the body and headed straight for her. He jumped up onto the bed straddling her body and placing his face right against hers.

"You are mine. I killed for you and you will love me like I love you in return. If you don't, and if the petals are right, then we both die, right here, today."

She couldn't believe that this was happening to her. She was so scared. She was shaking and didn't know what to do to get out of this. She had to stall him. She had to get him to think she was okay with this.

She sniffled as he leaned forward and licked her neck. His hands were groping her.

"Unc?" she whispered, voice quivering as he ran his hands up and down her arms that were tied to the top of the headboard.

He slowed his hands and then cupped her breasts as he sat up.

She licked her lips as tears continued to fall. "You really did all of that stuff you said, for me?"

He stared at her. She could count the number of breaths he took before he responded. Three, four, five. “Yes, all of it for you, for us, sweet little lover.”

He leaned forward and kissed her lips. She wanted to vomit, to bite him, kill him, and make him suffer. “I’m sorry I insulted you. I should have been more grateful. Paul hurt me so badly. I’m still so afraid.” She pretended to shiver. He ran his hands all over her and she had to pretend it didn’t repulse her.

“I’m sorry seeing him still upsets you, Ellie. That wasn’t my intention. He deserved to die. You shouldn’t feel bad. You should be grateful.”

“I am grateful. I want to hug you and thank you.”

He leaned down and pressed against her snugly.

“No, I mean with my own arms, I want to wrap them around you and hug you tight, and let you know that I appreciate everything that you did.” She clenched her eyes closed and prayed she wasn’t making matters worse for herself. As he pressed lower, she could see over his shoulder and through the open window. There were men in black. Someone was coming to save her.

“Please, Unc, untie me so I can hold you?”

“You want to hold me?”

“I want to, yes,” she whispered, tears flowing and out of her control.

He sat up, reached behind him and clicked the switch blade in front of her. She gasped and closed her eyes.

“What is it? What’s wrong?” he asked as he cut the first binding and then the other. She covered her face with her hands and willed herself to be strong, and she ignored the aches and pains from being tied up for so long.

“No knife. Please, I hate knives. Paul used a knife on me. Please, Unc, please get rid of it.”

“Of course. I forgot. I should have remembered that. It’s why I slit his throat for you. With this knife,” he said, showing it to her.

He stood up and placed it into his back pocket. She knelt on the bed, deciding where to run to, when suddenly there was a creak, a noise outside.

He grabbed her arm. "Someone is out there."

"No. I didn't hear anything. No one is there. Stay here with me. Let's talk. I want to know about all the plans and how you did it all. Stay here."

He grabbed her by the throat and lifted her up. She was kicking and holding on to his arm trying to get him to release her. Unc was crazy strong as she kicked and tried to free herself from his hold.

"You bitch. You're a liar, just like the others."

She shook her head, felt herself losing her last breath and about to pass out or die, when the doors burst open. The place filled with smoke and he dropped her. She fell to the floor, landing on her hand. She felt and heard the crack, but she was too occupied with trying to breathe. She was having difficulty, as she lay on her side, hearing the commotion, the cry of pain and then gunshots.

"Ellie! Goddamn it, Ellie!" Justice yelled out as he fell to his knees and pushed away her hair from her face.

"Baby, talk to me."

She held her wrist to her chest and still tried to breathe short breaths.

"She can't breathe. The fucker was choking her," Sam stated.

"I need a medic in here pronto. Look at this fucking mess," Gunny stated as he spoke into a radio on his bulletproof vest. There were men in black camo and bulletproof vests everywhere. Men in FBI jackets, police. The entire room was lit up. Justice picked her up and she cried, making it even harder to breathe.

"Shit, her wrist looks bad," Sam stated.

"Let me carry you out of this mess. You don't need to see any more, Ellie. It's over now," Justice told her.

"Unc?" she said and coughed.

"Dead," Justice told her as someone took off their FBI jacket and placed it over her body.

"Meet Gunner, Ellie. He's an old friend from the military."

He smiled, but he was a big man, and quite intimidating. "The ambulance is outside. We'll take care of everything. You take care of your woman," Gunner told them.

Justice gently picked her up into his arms and carried her out of the house.

* * * *

"Where the fuck is she? Do you think they were too late? Fuck, this waiting is killing me," Seno said.

"There. Holy shit, she's alive!" Mace yelled out, and he, Seno, and Hunter hurried to Justice and Ellie just as the paramedics directed him toward the gurney.

"Baby, thank God. Oh, thank God you're okay. I'm so sorry that I let him get you. I'm so sorry," Seno stated as he leaned down and kissed her cheek.

"She's hurt. Her wrist looks broken," Justice stated.

"And her neck? What are those marks on her?" Mace asked, looking concerned.

"What is she wearing?" Hunter asked, as they all took in the sight of the teddy. Seno felt like killing Unc again.

"I love you guys," she whispered and then cringed.

"We need to get her to the hospital."

"Let's go," Mace stated as they began to get the gurney up into the back of the ambulance.

"I'm sorry, but only one of you can fit in here," the paramedic stated.

"Seno, you go in the ambulance. Stay with her, and we'll meet you there," Justice told Seno. He nodded his head and got into the back of the ambulance with Ellie.

"Is it over, Justice? Is she safe now?" Hunter asked.

"Unc is dead. Sentinel, if he lives, is going away for a long time, and Paul can't ever hurt her again."

"Paul was in there?" Hunter asked.

"Unc killed Paul. I guess he kept his body around to show Ellie."

"Jesus, she's going to need us. All of us," Mace stated.

"And we need her. Let's go be with the woman we love," Justice said and smiled.

Chapter 14

Ellie opened her eyes to find Seno staring at her.

The last few days lying in bed trying to recover from everything had been a blur. Riding in the ambulance, seeing the tears in Seno's eyes, and knowing that he felt to blame for her abduction tore at her heart. Looking at him now, bloodshot eyes, a dark expression and lost look, she knew she needed to set the record straight. She had overheard Hunter and Justice talking about Seno wanting to write his resignation. He felt that he failed at his job and he failed her.

Hunter was asleep behind her, and she didn't know where Justice and Mace were. But she knew not far. They hadn't left her side.

"Okay, Seno, you need to get your shit together."

His eyes widened and he sat up on the side of the bed. "What do you mean?"

She sat up, being sure not to disturb Hunter, but knowing her men were retired soldiers, they all seemed like light sleepers. There wasn't much anyone could push past them.

She lifted the cast on her arm and rested it on her leg.

"I hope you weren't foolish enough to hand in your resignation and quit because of Unc?"

He turned to look at her. Well, more like glare at her. None of them liked mentioning Unc's name. Well, she didn't either, but this needed to be said.

"I should have recognized the signs. I should have noticed his personality that night in Ray Ray's. I ignored a gut instinct, Ellie. I'm a criminal analyst."

"Right. So in thirty minutes of meeting Unc, while we drank wine and joked around, you were supposed to look at him as a criminal? Sure, that makes total sense," she stated sarcastically.

He stood up and turned toward her, raising his voice. "You don't get it. I should have followed my gut and said no when he called to take you to lunch. I didn't like it. I didn't want him to. I knew something was wrong."

She stood up, wearing only an olive-green, marine T-shirt of Hunter's.

"You didn't want him to because you were jealous and being protective of what's yours. Listen, Seno, we all can go back and take a look at a lot of things we missed in many situations in our life. Hell, I knew the man for so many years and never once did the whole 'creepy guy' vibe go off. I trusted him with my life. Do you get that? He killed my uncle Brian. I had no idea. I never in a million years would have believed that, but it's true, and Unc told me. We mourned my uncle together. Unc was there for me after Paul assaulted me. Even months later, after counseling and everything, I still never got any vibe from him. That's not because I was naive, or blind, it was because Unc was that good at living a double life and deceiving all of us. You're not the first criminal analyst by profession to not recognize the signs of a criminal in your personal life. So get over it, and stop blaming yourself. I don't blame you. Your brothers don't blame you. So cut the shit, tear up the letter of resignation, and start focusing on this relationship and how much I love you and need you in my life."

He stomped toward her, pulled her into his arms, and immediately covered her bare ass with his palms. Squeezing them, she stood up on tiptoes and held his gaze.

"You sure you forgive me?"

"There's nothing to forgive, Seno. Now, take me to bed and make love to me. For some reason fighting with you guys makes me horny."

She heard the chuckles behind her as Seno lifted her up and brought her to the bed, laying her down on the edge.

As he parted her thighs with his palms and began to kiss her inner thighs, she looked back toward Hunter.

"Don't look so smug. You're next," she teased, and Seno licked between her pussy lips, making her gasp.

Despite her awkward cast, and her mental state of exhaustion, she felt reenergized and ready to make love to her men. Justice and Mace walked into the room, looking tired and asking what was going on, but neither she nor Seno answered as Seno continued to feast on her. As he thrust two fingers up into her cunt, she moaned and rocked her hips against them.

Seno stood up, pushed down his boxers, and aligned his cock with her pussy.

"Are you ready, baby?" he asked her.

"Always, Seno."

He stroked into her deeply, then lowered down so they were chest to chest as he cupped her face between his hands.

"I love you, Ellie, and my favorite place to be is inside of you, like this." He kissed her sweetly, as the others gathered on the bed around them, making her feel safe and loved. She knew in that moment that everything was perfect between the four of them. They each had their moments of insecurities, fears from their pasts, or just their dominant personalities as soldiers. But in the end, when that love was tested, when her own fears of letting another man into her heart after being hurt so deeply, these four men came through. Her American soldiers, her lovers, her best friends, her everything, finally made her life complete, and gave Ellie more than she ever dreamed about.

THE END

WWW.DIXIELYNNDWYER.COM

ABOUT THE AUTHOR

People seem to be more interested in my name than where I get my ideas for my stories from. So I might as well share the story behind my name with all my readers.

My momma was born and raised in New Orleans. At the age of twenty, she met and fell in love with an Irishman named Patrick Riley Dwyer. Needless to say, the family was a bit taken aback by this as they hoped she would marry a family friend. It was a modern day arranged marriage kind of thing and my momma downright refused.

Being that my momma's families were descendents of the original English speaking Southerners, they wanted the family blood line to stay pure. They were wealthy and my father's family was poor.

Despite attempts by my grandpapa to make Patrick leave and destroy the love between them, my parents married. They recently celebrated their sixtieth wedding anniversary.

I am one of six children born to Patrick and Lynn Dwyer. I am a combination of both Irish and a true Southern belle. With a name like Dixie Lynn Dwyer it's no wonder why people are curious about my name.

Just as my parents had a love story of their own, I grew up intrigued by the lifestyles of others. My imagination as well as my need to stray from the straight and narrow made me into the woman I am today.

For all titles by Dixie Lynn Dwyer, please visit
www.bookstrand.com/dixie-lynn-dwyer

Siren Publishing, Inc.
www.SirenPublishing.com

Lightning Source UK Ltd.
Milton Keynes UK
UKHW02f1556110418
320862UK00006B/847/P